THE TEXAS TATTLER

All the news that's barely fit to print!

Fortune Love Triangle Revealed

Undercover sources report that alleged murderess Lily Cassidy recently made an earth-shattering cellblock confession to fawning fiancé Ryan Fortune: He isn't the first Fortune tycoon to share her bed. While working as a housekeeper on the Double Crown Ranch over thirty years ago, Lily was seduced by treacherous playboy Cameron Fortune, Ryan's now-deceased older brother. Bombshell number two: She bore a secret Fortune son, thirty-five-year-old lawyer Cole Cassidy!

Ryan, forever true to Lily and horribly lonely since his beloved's incarceration, continues to barrage the jailhouse with chocolates, roses and...hey, is there a legal *file* in that fancy French pastry?

Rumor has it that Lily's defense team, her son, Cole, and private eye Annie Jones, have met before and are intimately familiar with various "crimes of passion." This duo has some mighty unusual investigative tactics—like forging marriage certificates with their own names. Someone please tell these two that they need to come out from *under* the covers in order to *go* undercover....

About the Author

PAMELA TOTH

USA TODAY bestselling author Pamela Toth was born
in Wisconsin, but grew up in Seattle, where she
attended the University of Washington and majored in
art. Now living on the Puget Sound area's east side, she
has two daughters, Erika and Melody, and two Siamese
cats.

Recently she took a lead from one of her own
romances and married her high school sweetheart,
Frank. They live in a town house within walking
distance of a bookstore and an ice-cream shop, two
of life's necessities, with a fabulous view of Mount
Rainier. When she's not writing, she enjoys traveling
with her husband, reading, playing FreeCell on the
computer, doing counted cross-stitch and researching
new story ideas. She's been an active member of
Romance Writers of America since 1982.

Her books have won several awards and they claim a
regular spot on the Waldenbooks bestselling romance
list. She loves hearing from readers and can be reached
at P.O. Box 5845, Bellevue, WA 98006. For a personal
reply, a stamped, self-addressed envelope is appreciated.

PAMELA TOTH
Wedlocked?!

Published by Silhouette Books

America's Publisher of Contemporary Romance

Special thanks and acknowledgment are given to Pamela Toth for her contribution to THE FORTUNES OF TEXAS series.

 SILHOUETTE BOOKS

ISBN 0-373-38924-8

WEDLOCKED?!

This edition published by arrangement with Harlequin Books S.A.

® and TM are trademarks of Harlequin Books S.A., used under license. Trademarks indicated with ® are registered in the United States Patent and Trademark Office, the Canadian Trade Marks Office and in other countries.

Visit Silhouette Books at www.eHarlequin.com

Printed in U.S.A.

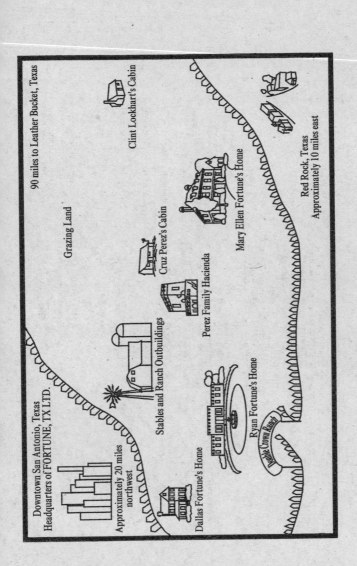

THE FORTUNES OF TEXAS

KINGSTON FORTUNE (d)

1st marriage
PATIENCE TALBOT (d)

Teddy §

2nd marriage
SELENA HOBBS (d)

CAMERON (d)
m MARY ELLEN LOCKHART

RYAN
1st marriage
JANINE LOCKHART (d)

2nd marriage
SOPHIA BARNES

MIRANDA
m Lloyd Carter (D)

KANE GABRIELLE ⑧
m
Wyatt Grayhawk

VICTORIA ⑩
m
Quinn McCoy

HOLDEN ① LOGAN ⑤ EDEN ⑦
m   m   m
Lucinda Amanda   Sheikh
Brightwater Sue*   Ben Ramir

m Emily Applegate

LILY REDGROVE   Sawyer*

MATTHEW ZANE ⑫
m
Claudia Beaumont

Bryan

DALLAS ④ VANESSA ② ***VICTORIA ⑩
1st marriage m   m
Sara Andersen (d) Devin Kincaid
2nd marriage m
Maggie Perez

† ROSITA and RUBEN PEREZ

Anita Carmen Frieda

CRUZ ③
m
Savannah Clark

MAGGIE ④
1st marriage
m
Craig Randall (D)

Travis
2nd marriage
m
Dallas Fortune

CLINT LOCKHART
brother of
JACE LOCKHART ⑥
m
Clara Wilde

HANNAH ⑨ MARIA
m   m
Parker   James a.k.a.
Malone   Taylor

COLE* ⑪
m
Chester Cassidy (d)

TITLES:

1. MILLION DOLLAR MARRIAGE
2. THE BABY PURSUIT
3. EXPECTING...IN TEXAS
4. A WILLING WIFE
5. CORPORATE DADDY
6. SNOWBOUND CINDERELLA
7. THE SHEIKH'S SECRET SON
8. THE HEIRESS AND THE SHERIFF
9. LONE STAR WEDDING
10. IN THE ARMS OF A HERO
11. WEDLOCKED?!
12. HIRED BRIDE

---

*   Child of affair
d   Deceased
D   Divorced
m   Married
*** Twins
†   Loyal ranch staff
§   Kidnapped by maternal grandfather

THE FORTUNES OF TEXAS™

 **Meet the Fortunes of Texas**

Cole Cassidy: He would do anything to catch the person who'd framed his mother for murder—even team up with his former lover, investigator Annie Jones....

Annie Jones: Cole was the last person Annie ever wanted to see again, let alone work with! She'd been burned once by Cole and refused to fall in love with him again. But some things were beyond her control....

Maria Cassidy: Cole's youngest sister's zealous interest in babies has the family talking. Will Maria's secrets be safe much longer?

Zane Fortune: The executive heartbreaker has just about every blue-blooded beauty in Texas at his feet. However, not one of those socialites has captured his attention quite as much as a certain down-on-her-luck single mom....

This book is dedicated to my fellow alumni of Blanchet High School in Seattle, class of '65, with the hope that your lives have all been as happy and fulfilling as mine. The best is yet to come.

And to Frank Bell, class of '64, who puts the romance in my writing and in my life.

One

"You aren't going to prison," Cole Cassidy promised the woman seated across the table from him. Even though their relationship had recently become strained, Lily was still his mother. "I'll do everything I can to clear you."

Lily abandoned her surveillance of the restaurant's entry long enough to glance at Cole. The pressure of the last few weeks had left shadows beneath her dark eyes, but she was still a beautiful woman.

"You believe that I didn't murder Sophia Fortune, don't you?" she asked, an uncharacteristic quaver in her husky voice. "I swear I'm telling the truth."

Cole leaned forward and squeezed her hand. It was icy cold. "I know you're innocent," he replied. "You don't have to convince me."

"The prisons are full of innocent people." Her fingers shifted restlessly as she waited for the arrival of her fiancé, Ryan Fortune. He was bringing with him the private investigator he'd hired to dig up enough evidence to clear Lily of the murder charge for which she was out on bail.

Cole wanted to reassure his mother, to tell her he knew she would never lie to him. Yet she had lied—repeatedly—by omission, and that knowledge stood between them like an elephant both were pretending they couldn't see.

Before he could think of something to say about her honesty that wouldn't reek of irony, Lily's attention was diverted. Recognition hummed through the room as her fiancé, the head of the Fortune empire and owner of the Double Crown Ranch, stopped in the entryway. As soon as he spotted Lily, his weathered face relaxed into a smile. Then, as Cole got to his feet, Ryan leaned down and spoke to the woman at his side.

As the two of them came toward Cole's table, identification and disbelief double-teamed him, driving the air from his chest like a one–two punch to the gut.

Lily glanced up. "Is something wrong?"

Her voice was nearly drowned out by the sudden roaring in Cole's ears. It couldn't be—and yet it was. The riot of brown curls, the heart-shaped face and those wide, kissable lips—the image was seared into his memory like the scar from a red-hot branding iron.

The woman with Ryan was Annie Jones, the same woman Cole had left behind six years before when he'd moved to Denver.

The moment Annie recognized the tall, dark-haired man waiting for Ryan, an icy hand squeezed her heart with painful ferocity. Pride was all that kept her from stopping dead in her tracks.

Ryan must have sensed her hesitation as he led her to the table. "Lily and her son make a handsome pair, don't they?" he asked. Without waiting for a reply, he leaned over to give the woman with Cole Cassidy a quick kiss on her upturned mouth.

If the man who'd hired Annie had been anyone else in the Lone Star state, no matter how wealthy, powerful or well-connected, she would have ditched the case and walked away. Unfortunately, she owed Ryan Fortune far too much to even consider letting him down. Since quitting wasn't an option, she straightened her spine, curved her mouth into a cool smile and did her best to mask the turmoil scrambling her insides like a butter churn.

"Hello, Cole," she said before Ryan could begin the introductions. "How have you been?" For good measure, Annie extended her hand.

If her calm demeanor surprised him, Annie's former lover gave no sign except a slight narrowing of his piercing blue eyes—eyes that had once burned with an intense yet shallow desire Annie had briefly mistaken for love.

It was a mistake she hadn't made since.

After a pause so slight that she might have imagined it, Cole enfolded her hand in his. She felt his touch all the way to the heart she would have sworn had turned to stone after he'd walked out on her. Before she could even begin to absorb the heat and strength of his grip, he released her. His expression was somber, without even the hint of a smile, and he met her generic greeting with silence.

"You already know each other?" Ryan asked.

His tone made Annie curious, and she filed it away for future analysis. Right now she was too busy dealing with a situation she had both dreaded and fantasized about—meeting Cole again. "We haven't seen each other for years," she told Ryan with a bland smile before she shifted her attention to the woman seated at the table.

"You must be Lily. Ryan's told me about you." Although Cole had mentioned his mother to her frequently during their former association, the two women had never met. Annie had no idea Cole's mother and Ryan's fiancée were one and the same.

Silently, Annie congratulated herself on the steadiness of her own voice, and hoped the heat searing her cheeks didn't glow like Rudolph's nose. Determined that Cole glimpse not a hint of her inner agitation, she concentrated instead on the older woman studying her with a thoughtful expression.

Lily Cassidy had the dark hair and compelling looks that were a legacy of the Spanish and Apache heritage she shared with her son. No wonder Ryan Fortune had been willing to endure an expensive and very public divorce from the woman Lily now stood accused of murdering. Ryan's intended was still as striking as her son was handsome.

Too bad the last six years had been so kind to

Cole as well. Annie would have taken some small measure of satisfaction in seeing that his hairline had receded, his waist had expanded or the clean line of his jaw had begun to blur. Instead he'd grown more attractive since the day he had walked away from her without a backward glance. Had some other woman managed to do what Annie had not—capture his heart and his name?

Sometimes life just wasn't fair, Annie thought, and then she recalled why she was here. Cole's mother had been accused of murder. Her life wasn't all fun and games. Neither, obviously, was Cole's.

"Ryan speaks highly of you," Lily said. "Please won't you sit down?"

Deliberately Annie ignored the chair Cole pulled out, choosing instead the one on Lily's other side. The strain of the last few weeks was evident in her expression, but there was warmth in her eyes, and barely visible laugh lines framing her mouth.

Annie was no Mary Poppins. She'd been a cop and she'd seen the worst in people. Appearances were often deceiving, yet she felt a burst of empathy toward Cole's mother. Annie knew what it was like to be wrongly accused. Whether her empathy with Lily was misplaced remained to be seen.

"How well did you and Cole know each other?" Ryan asked, taking the fourth chair across the table.

A waiter handed Annie a menu, which she immediately opened. "Not well at all," she said dismissively.

Lily looked at her son. Apparently she had a mother's keen awareness when it came to undercurrents. "Cole?" she asked.

"We lost touch when I moved to Denver," he said in a tone that didn't invite more questions. He had taken refuge in his own menu and his expression was grim. Unfortunately for Annie, the slight frown did nothing to mar his attractiveness. Nor her own response to him—one that up until a few minutes before she would have sworn she'd managed to put far, far behind her. How disgustingly pathetic to feel such tingling awareness of the rat who had accepted her guilt when she'd so desperately needed him, of all people, to believe in her innocence.

Just like he wanted her to believe in his mother's innocence now. The irony of the situation made Annie blink, and then she realized that all three of her companions were staring at her expectantly.

"Excuse me?" she asked, fresh heat bathing her cheeks.

Cole's frown deepened. "I was just asking Ryan why he'd chosen you to investigate my mother's case. You're young and relatively inexperienced. There are plenty more seasoned P.I.'s in San Antonio." How like an attorney to grab the offensive.

"And I was about to explain to Cole that age doesn't necessarily indicate ability. Annie's bright, sharp and aggressive. When it comes to clearing the woman I love, I want the very best available on our team." Ryan reached across the table to clasp Lily's outstretched hand. To Annie's surprise, fresh tears sprang to the other woman's dark eyes.

"Thank you, my love." Her voice vibrated with emotion.

Pain sliced through Annie as she glanced away from the mutual trust and affection the brief exchange revealed. It was obvious that Ryan's belief in Lily's innocence was total. If only Cole could have been as sure of Annie's years before.

For a moment, her gaze collided with his and she wondered if he could read her thoughts. A muscle ticked in his cheek, but he didn't look away this time. It was Annie who finally raised her brows and managed to break the deadlock as the waiter approached. Her heart was racing. In the few moments it took the man to gather their orders, she was able to regain her poise and put the painful memories where they belonged.

Despite the lurid coverage of the tabloid press, the circumstances of Sophia Fortune's murder left plenty of room for speculation. Smothering someone with a pillow was a very up-close and personal crime, not like shooting the victim from several yards away. Annie wondered if the woman seated across from her was capable of that kind of in-your-face violence. The case would be a fascinating one to investigate.

"What makes you think Ms. Jones is the best investigator available?" Cole asked Ryan.

Annie had no intention of losing this opportunity

just because her presence made him uncomfortable. As his mother's attorney, Cole would have to work with her on the investigation. If he wanted her fired, he was going to have to admit to Ryan, and his mother, why.

Before Annie could open her mouth, though, the waiter brought the iced teas they had all ordered. As he retreated, Ryan spoke directly to Cole. He must have sensed that the son would be a harder sell than the mother.

"Living in Denver, you may not be aware of the solid reputation Annie's built for herself all through this part of Texas," Ryan said. "I guess it must have been after your move that she left the police department, despite the protests of her superior officers, and opened her own agency."

Surprise flickered across Cole's face. Apparently he'd never bothered to find out the outcome of the charges filed against her within the department. This fresh evidence of his indifference to her fate hurt like hell.

"Since then she's done some brilliant work on several difficult, high-profile cases." Ryan turned his attention to Lily. "Honey, believe me, if anyone can give Cole the strongest ammunition to get you an acquittal, Annie can."

Annie felt like squirming with embarrassment in the face of Ryan's testimonial. Granted, she'd worked damn hard after her tattered reputation had been restored and she'd left the department. She'd still had a lot to prove—to her late father and to the people who had believed she'd disgraced both his memory and the badge he'd worn with pride. Case by difficult case, she'd earned her reputation and the hefty fees she now charged. Even so, Ryan's wholesale endorsement made her uncomfortable. What if this time—when it mattered to him the most—she failed?

Lily took a sip of her iced tea and turned to look at Annie. "I suppose you know about the charges against me?"

Annie nodded. Anyone who hadn't been lost in the wilderness knew Lily's story. Since Ryan's phone call, Annie had boned up on the case.

"Let me see if I've got it right," she replied, deliberately pulling no punches. "The police think you killed Sophia because her refusal to give Ryan a divorce was preventing you from bagging one of the wealthiest men in the state." She ignored Ryan's gasp. "You had means, opportunity and motive, since you just happened to be staying at her hotel in Austin on the night in question. You told the police you hadn't been in her suite, but they found your bracelet on the floor by her body. They say the two of you quarreled and you held a pillow over her face until she was dead."

During Annie's recital, Lily had paled, but she seemed to draw strength from Ryan. Her chin went up. "I didn't do it. I could never take another per-

son's life.'' Her gaze held Annie's without waver-
ing. ''Do you believe me?''

Annie noticed that Cole had shifted closer to his
mother as if to protect her. Where had all that loving
support been when *she'd* needed it? ''I don't have
to believe you to do my job,'' she told Lily.

Angrily Cole slapped his hand on the table, making them jump. He had no intention of sitting quietly
while this hotshot P.I. tried and convicted his mother
of murder right here in the restaurant. Annie's bald
recital of both the facts and speculation surrounding
the case had just handed him a concrete excuse to
refuse to work with her on the investigation.

''I've heard enough,'' he told Ryan, confident the
older man would agree with him. ''We'll have to
find someone else.''

To his surprise, his mother gripped his arm. ''No,
dear, I don't think so.''

Cole knew that tone. Underneath the soft drawl
lay pure steel. Still he argued. ''You need someone
who knows you're innocent.''

She shook her head, a rueful smile curving her
lips. ''I have you and Ryan for that,'' she said hus-
kily. Then she looked right at Annie. ''Miss Jones,
I need a fighter on my side. I'd like you to take my
case. If Ryan says you're good, that's enough for
me.''

Cole's automatic protest died in his throat. Under
the circumstances, surely Annie would refuse.

Instead she smiled. Despite his annoyance, Cole

felt his nerves leap in reaction. Working with her would be insane—just one of several reasons why she had no business on this case, but the one he could never verbalize. And what about the resentment she might still feel toward him over the past? What better revenge than standing by and watching his mother go to prison? Could the Annie he'd known have turned into the kind of person who would let something that evil happen—even contribute to it? Could he risk the possibility?

Before he could bring up his other objections, the waiter was back with their food. Grimly, Cole realized he might have better luck discussing the situation with Ryan and his mother later, away from Annie's troubling presence.

As Ryan turned the conversation away from the case, Cole concentrated on his lobster salad and tried to resist sneaking peeks at the woman seated across from him, the thick brown hair he remembered so well pulled into a high ponytail that made her look younger than her twenty-nine years. He didn't know which of the emotions churning through him was more disturbing—his guilt over the way he'd handled their breakup, the renewed attraction to her that threatened his focus now, or the certainty that being thrown together on this case would be a disaster not only for him but also for his mother, whose very life was on the line.

"I can take a cab," Annie said, wanting nothing more than to get away from Cole long enough to catch her breath and beat her overactive hormones back into submission. Not that she was the least bit interested in him—she'd learned her lesson there— but a woman could admire a man on a strictly physical level as long as it didn't interfere with the work at hand.

"Nonsense," Ryan replied with the breezy confidence of the super-rich. "The ranch is in the opposite direction from your office, and Lily needs to rest. But Cole can drop you off." His arm was curved protectively around Lily's shoulders. "It will afford the two of you a chance to map out your strategy."

Even Annie couldn't argue with that. It was time to put aside her personal feelings toward her new client's son and get busy. They had barely a month until the trial, and there was a lot to be done.

She glanced at Cole, who was watching her with an unreadable expression on his sharply chiseled face. Did he never relax these days? She remembered that he had a killer smile. The unfortunate memory jarred her back to reality.

"Good idea," she agreed with a hint of challenge in her voice. "If you have time to get started right away, so do I."

The flicker of surprise in Cole's eyes was more than enough reward for her capitulation. "My mother's out on bail," he drawled. "I don't have a lot else on my calendar right now."

Moments later, the two couples had split up, the older pair heading for the car Ryan's driver had brought around to the front door of the restaurant. Meanwhile, Cole led the way to the lot behind the building where his rental was parked. If his back were any straighter, Annie might have suspected his tailor had sewed a metal rod in his jacket.

"So how have you been?" she asked, striving for a light tone, after he'd joined her in the confines of his white Lexus. The interior reeked of leather and wealth. Her ancient Volkswagen smelled like pine cleaner, courtesy of a dangling piece of cardboard shaped like an evergreen tree.

She refused to analyze why it was important that he see how easily she was handling his sudden reappearance in her life. She just knew she wanted to get the preliminaries out of the way so they could concentrate on the case.

Cole backed the car out of its parking spot and headed toward the street. "I've been fine," he said as he eased into a break in traffic. "I don't know if you'd heard that I moved to Denver after—"

"I heard," she blurted, and then could have bitten off her tongue for her unguarded response. He'd probably think she'd tracked him like a spurned lover who didn't know when to let go. She couldn't remember who had told her, but she damn well couldn't explain that she hadn't sought out the information, not without looking ridiculous. This was going to be more difficult than she'd realized.

The light turned red, and Cole took the opportunity to really look at her. Nearly hidden by her air of self-confidence and the solid reputation Ryan had described lurked a freshness that was downright amazing. Life had handed her lemons and from them she'd made a blue-ribbon pie. When he recalled how thoroughly he'd misjudged her, he wanted to turn back the clock and rewrite history.

"Look," he said instead as the light changed and the cars in front of him began to move, "we probably need to clear the air. Can we wait to discuss our history together until we get to your office before I rear-end someone?"

He sensed her sudden tension. Maybe she wasn't as indifferent to him as she would like him to think, or maybe it was just resentment that had her hands tightening on her patchwork leather bag. Again he wondered how far she might go to avenge herself. Would she punish an innocent woman? Damage her own reputation as an investigator? He had to admit the possibility was pretty far-fetched—and damn egotistical of him.

"There's really nothing to discuss," she said in a voice that had plunged several degrees in temperature despite the heat of the October day. "At least nothing of a personal nature. We have a lot of ground to cover for your mother's case. I suggest we focus on the present and forget ancient history."

"If that's the way you want it," Cole muttered, swerving and hitting his horn when a car in the next

lane cut them off. The other driver didn't appear to
notice.

For the next few moments, Cole's attention was
divided between the directions she gave him and
speculation about what she must really be feeling.
The former was straightforward enough; her expression yielded no clues to the latter. Finally they
turned into a small strip mall and he stopped the car
beside a faded blue bug with a hot-pink windsock
attached to its antenna.

In front of them was a rather plain storefront with
simple black lettering on the glass door. Annie
Jones, Private Investigator, it read, followed by a
local phone number. Her office was flanked by a dry
cleaner on one side and a hobby shop on the other.
Its grimy window was filled with a stack of faded
cardboard boxes, the type plastic model kits come
in, and dead flies. Neither business bordering hers
looked especially prosperous.

Cole was trying to think of a comment—something neutral—when Annie got out of the car without a word and unlocked the front door of her office.

"Coming?" she demanded when he made no
move to follow her.

Flushing, he grabbed his briefcase from behind
the seat, locked the rental carefully and went inside.
He didn't know what he'd expected, but not the
comfortable clutter that greeted him. With painful
clarity, he pictured the tiny, cheerful apartment

she'd had before—shabby, eclectic and welcoming. In some ways, Annie hadn't changed.

"Have a seat," she told him as she grabbed a stack of manila folders from a chair facing a scarred metal desk, and dumped them on top of a file cabinet. "I'll just be a minute." Sitting down behind the desk, she picked up the phone.

While she checked her voice mail, Cole cleared a spot in front of him for his briefcase and took the opportunity to look around. Modern computer equipment shared space with battered file cabinets and crammed bookcases. On the one bare wall were several framed citations. Cole figured he'd better wait to examine them more closely. On another wall was a calendar still turned to the month before. On the counter were two dirty coffee cups and an apothecary jar filled with lemon drops. Annie might be as organized as a surgical team, but neatness wasn't any more of a priority now than it had ever been.

Cole wondered if he could work in the midst of such clutter. The top of his own desk in Denver was always bare except for his current project. His files and baskets were color-coordinated, his books shelved according to subject and cataloged on his computer.

Now he looked at the self-stick notes dotting the side of the computer monitor and sighed.

The closing of a drawer drew his attention back to the woman seated across from him. She'd taken out a yellow legal pad and uncapped a cheap pen.

"Let's start from the beginning," she said, her gaze boring into him as though she were about to interview a suspect. "Tell me everything you know about the case."

For the first time in a long while, Annie could find no peace, no relaxation in the condominium she'd taken such pleasure in decorating the year before. Even her cat, rescued from a shelter to become Annie's number one fan, failed to distract her from her thoughts tonight. It had been a long afternoon, going over the facts of Lily Cassidy's case with Cole and planning her strategy to poke holes in the state's theory of how and why the crime had been committed. All they needed for an acquittal was reasonable doubt.

"Not now, Sluggo," Annie murmured distractedly when the cat jumped into her lap and began butting his wide head against her hand. Gently she deposited him back on the carpeted floor, barely aware of his sharp *meow* of protest. Devoted he might be, but the big orange tabby was also unused to being ignored. Annie knew she'd have to placate him later for the slight she'd dealt his pride.

No matter. There were too many thoughts chasing each other around in her head for her to be able to focus on her cat, the Celine Dion CD she'd put on her stereo, or the glass of Merlot she'd poured herself when she'd first gotten home.

It was obvious that Cole didn't want her on the

case, and just as obvious that both his mother and Ryan did. For the last reason, and because Annie knew what it was like to be wrongly accused, she'd ignored Cole's lack of enthusiasm toward her over lunch and accepted the assignment. She hoped that neither she nor Lily Cassidy would live to regret it.

With a sigh, Annie opened the denim tote she used in lieu of a briefcase and removed the notes she'd made that afternoon. Once they'd gotten started, she and Cole had covered a lot of ground. His memory for detail was phenomenal. They'd worked well together, their thought processes operating in a similar fashion that eliminated lengthy explanations between them. Indeed, they'd each picked up on what the other had been trying to communicate with a speed that reminded Annie painfully of the way they'd meshed six years ago. Sometimes back then words hadn't been necessary at all, just touch and taste—

Annie leaped to her feet, scattering papers and scaring the cat, who ran behind the couch. This was getting her nowhere! Taking a deep breath and letting it out slowly through her mouth, she gathered up her notes and sat back down. Kicking off her shoe, she tucked her foot beneath her, sipped her wine and stared at her own barely legible handwriting.

She would have liked to ask Cole about his life in Denver. She was curious as heck about what he'd been doing for the last six years, but she wouldn't admit it—not to him. No, the last thing she wanted to hear was how, up in Colorado, he'd found the perfect woman, or, even worse, a whole string of perfect women to keep him company.

He wasn't wearing a ring, but she knew that didn't mean anything. Would Ryan have mentioned whether Cole was married? No, there was no reason for that—just as there was no room for personal feelings here. Not anger, not bitterness and certainly not regret. No matter how she felt about Cole, she knew what it was like to face the endless stares and questions from people who'd already decided you were guilty, all the while wondering if your life would ever be the same.

It made not the slightest difference that the woman facing a similar ordeal was the mother of the man who'd walked out when Annie had needed him desperately, ripping out her heart as he went. How satisfying to be instrumental in getting Lily Cassidy off, and in knowing that from now on her son would owe Annie for something he could never hope to repay. When he thought of her, the feelings in his heart would be obligation and gratitude, however reluctantly given, and not the somewhat distant indifference he'd shown her today.

Two

"Where have you been?" Cole asked Annie as soon as the temp he'd hired had shown her into his borrowed office and departed, closing the door behind her. "I expected to hear from you before this." He picked up the gold pen his father had given him upon graduation from law school and rolled it between his fingers.

Not his biological father, Cole reminded himself with a wry twist of his lips, just the man who'd raised him like a son. The man he'd believed to be his real father until just a few weeks ago.

"It's only been two days," Annie replied, dropping her purse and a denim bag on the floor next to an empty leather chair. "I had things to do." Gone was the trim gray power suit she'd worn with a white blouse and button earrings at lunch the other day. Only her hair was the same, piled into a curly mass on top of her head.

Silver hoops dangled from her ears and sparkled when she turned her head. A blue sweater hugged her breasts and barely covered her midriff. Snug jeans, the fabric bleached nearly white and fraying around the pockets, and thick-soled sandals completed her outfit.

She followed the direction of Cole's gaze. "My field uniform," she said with a saucy little shimmy of her hips.

Cole nearly stepped on his tongue. Next to her, he felt overdressed and stodgy. Irritated, he straightened the knot of his tie. "Now that you're here," he said, tapping the folder in front of him, "I want to go over this paperwork with you."

Instead of plopping obediently into a chair, Annie hooked her thumbs into her pockets and glanced around the small room. "Nice digs," she murmured, turning back to face him. Lightly, she ran her finger over a jade panther that rested on the corner of his desk. That and a brass lamp with a Tiffany-style glass shade were Cole's. He'd brought them from Denver. The only other items on the desk were the file he'd been studying, a legal pad and a phone with an intercom. Clutter was distracting. He thought of Annie's office and shuddered.

"My soon-to-be brother-in-law loaned me the office space," Cole said. "Parker's engaged to my sister Hannah, and he's been handling Dad's divorce."

Before Cole had moved in here, the room had been used for storage. Bookcases full of legal tomes covered two walls and a row of mismatched file cabinets lined a third. Cartons of printer paper were stacked in one corner. At least there was a small window behind him with a view of the sky and the busy street below.

"How long are you staying in Texas?" Annie asked.

"Until the trial's over." He lined the pen up next to the pad of paper. Behind him, the air conditioner hummed quietly. "Let's get to work." In the last two days, he'd been torn between worry over his mother and endless speculation about Annie. How much had she changed? Was she as confident as she appeared? Was she still passionate about her work? Had she ever given him a thought in the last six years? Did she hate him? Thanks to his future step-father, Cole might have to work with Annie, but he'd be damned if he'd let her know he still found her attractive.

Finally she sat down, crossed one leg over the other and fished a manila folder from her bag. "Did you know that Ryan's wife was having an affair before she died?"

Interest surged through Cole. He knew his mother hadn't murdered Sophia, which meant that someone else had—someone angry enough to press a pillow to her face until she stopped breathing. A spurned lover? An obsessed reject? From what Ryan had already told Cole, his estranged wife had certainly been capable of a secret involvement with someone else while she did her best to squeeze a bigger settlement from her husband.

"I heard rumors," Cole admitted. "Have you found out who the lucky man was?"

To his disappointment, Annie shook her head. "Not yet, but I will."

"What have you been doing all this time?" he demanded, frustrated.

She gave him a level stare. "Working. How about you? Established a foolproof defense yet?"

Her sarcastic tone made him realize that the two of them sniping at each other wasn't going to help his mother's case. "I'm sorry," he muttered. "I'm worried." He glanced at the thick file he'd been reading before she came in. "I've been going over the police report from the crime scene," he added. "The only physical evidence that ties Mom to the scene was the ruby bracelet they found next to the body. It was a gift from Ryan. Someone else had to have deliberately planted it in Sophia's hotel room. Mom was never there."

"Are you sure of that?" Annie asked.

Cole fought down his protective urges. "She says she wasn't. That's good enough for me."

"But not necessarily good enough to convince a jury," Annie pointed out. "Why would anyone want to frame her?"

"To divert attention, I suppose," he replied. "Because Mom was at the hotel that night and she knew Sophia. Anyone could have seen her there."

Annie twirled a lock of her hair, and he noticed that she wore a ring shaped like a butterfly. Her nails were short, neat and free of polish. "What about the bracelet?" she asked. "Did the police talk to anyone who thought they remembered her wearing it that night?"

Cole thought for a moment. "I don't think so. Good point."

Annie made a note. "I'll check it out. Why was Lily at the hotel that night?"

He sat back and steepled his hands, the leather of his chair creaking in protest like an old saddle. "She attended a charity banquet at the hotel and, unfortunately for her, she decided to stay the night."

Annie pursed her lips thoughtfully. "What's her alibi for the time when Sophia was killed?" she asked.

"She was in her own room," Cole admitted with a sigh. "Alone."

"No room service? No phone calls?" Annie probed with a wave of her hand.

He shook his head regretfully. "She was resting."

Annie appeared to be studying the scenic print behind his head. He tried to stay focused on the discussion and not notice how full her lips were, puckered as if for a kiss. Did she have a boyfriend?

"I think our best bet would be to find out who Sophia was involved with," she said as he tried hard to concentrate. "I'm not usually a fan of putting the victim on trial, but it wouldn't hurt to alter a jury's image of her as the wronged wife."

Cole couldn't fault Annie's reasoning. From the

beginning, publicity surrounding the case had played up its sensational aspects. Anything connected to the wealthy Fortune family was big news in Texas. "Good idea. Where do we start?"

Annie leaned back and studied him pointedly. The movement thrust out her breasts. Memories had his fingers curling in reaction behind the desk. "We?" she echoed.

"She's my mother," he replied a little more forcefully than necessary. "I'm not just some attorney trying to better his win–loss record."

"Precisely. You're biased."

"And you're not?" he countered.

"I haven't formed an opinion of her guilt or innocence yet, if that's what you mean," she said loftily.

Cole ignored the quick surge of temper. "Why did you take this case?" he asked instead.

Her gaze didn't waver. "Ryan Fortune has been very supportive," she said finally. "I owe him."

Cole narrowed his eyes. "Is that the only reason?"

She shifted in her chair and uncrossed her legs. "What are you implying?"

"You can't ignore the fact that you and I have a history," Cole said with great reluctance. He hadn't meant to bring it up, but maybe it would be better to clear the air now, before they got deeper into the investigation.

Annie was surprised he would mention their unfortunate past. "Ancient history." She bristled at the idea that he might think she'd let anything personal influence the way she handled a case. "It certainly has no bearing on this investigation." She didn't like the way he was studying her, but she refused to allow him to put her on the defensive. Instead she leaned down to stuff the folder back into her bag, then got to her feet.

"I'll keep you posted." Before she could reach the door, Cole had circled his desk and blocked her path. She could smell his cologne. Thank heaven he'd changed brands and the new scent, something clean and sharp, wasn't another painful reminder of the past they'd shared.

"I'm sorry," he said softly, easing his hands into the pockets of his gray slacks and propping his shoulder against the door. "Can we start over?" He was so close she could see the faint stubble of his beard, could feel his breath on her cheek.

"No problem." Annie refused to retreat. Instead she looked into his eyes, at the twin reflections of herself in the blackness of his pupils, as awareness—stronger than a sigh but fainter than a whisper—shimmered between them.

Cole was the first to step away, leaving her to wonder if he felt it too. He gave his silk tie, the exact same blue as his irises, an unnecessary tug, but his expression remained unchanged.

Annie realized she'd die if he suspected she still found him attractive. She felt like a dog that had been kicked and kept crawling back to its master no matter how many times it was hurt.

"Let's start by pooling our information," Cole suggested briskly, sliding the folder around so it was facing the chair she'd just vacated. "Here's the police report."

Curious, Annie sat back down and did her best to concentrate on the form in front of her. "How odd," she murmured when she'd scanned the report of the crime scene.

Cole perched on the corner of the desk. "What do you mean?"

"As usual, there was a lot of physical evidence to sift through—fingerprints, hair, fibers." She glanced over the report. "I know this forensics team," she said, tapping the paper for emphasis. "If there had been anything else in that hotel room to link your mother to the victim, no matter how minuscule, they should have found it." She looked again. "They have several unidentified fingerprints, but none of Lily's." Perhaps Lily was telling the truth.

"Of course they don't have her prints. She wasn't there," Cole insisted. "Maybe something will match up to the real killer."

Annie ignored his comment. "What else do you have?" she asked, pulling a bag of lemon drops from her bag and holding them out. Did he remember how he used to buy them for her?

Declining her offer, he sat back down and shuffled through more papers. "Witness statements. A copy of the hotel registry. The autopsy report." He frowned. "The police believe the only two acquaintances of Sophia's who were at the hotel the night of the murder were Lily and the ranch employee who drove her there, Roy Dirkson."

"What do we know about Dirkson?" Annie asked eagerly.

Cole kept reading. "He's in the clear. He was seen having a beer in the bar after he dropped Mom at the hotel, and he swears he left right after that. A couple of witnesses corroborated his statement. I suppose he could have circled around and come back to the hotel later, but, judging by how soon he got to the ranch, he's probably telling the truth."

"His arrival time is documented too?" Annie asked.

"By Ryan himself. Dirkson reported to him when he arrived."

Sucking on the lemon drop, she made a note on the pad she'd pulled out. "I'll talk to Dirkson again before we eliminate him," she decided.

Cole's brows lifted. "It can't hurt, but what reason could he possibly have had to kill her?" he asked skeptically.

"From what I've learned so far about dear Sophia," Annie felt compelled to explain, "her taste in men was eclectic. Dirkson's worth a look." She'd be darned if she was going to justify every step she took to Cole.

"Anything else?" she asked.

"Only that Sophia's hotel room showed definite signs of a struggle, and Mom had no scratches or bruising on her arms or face when they questioned her," he replied.

Annie made another note and drew a star next to it. "How do the police explain that? Sophia must have fought back."

He shrugged. "They don't even try. I'll have Tiffany make copies of all this for you." He pressed a button on his intercom.

When his secretary opened the door and he rose to hand her the file, Annie took the opportunity to study him from beneath her lashes. His suit was impeccably tailored, his black shoes as shiny as tinted windows. He had always liked to dress well.

If she didn't put the past where it belonged, this case was only going to be more difficult. As it was, Lily had already been tried and found guilty in the press, which had painted her as a gold digger, a home-wrecker and worse. The obvious holes in the case wouldn't matter to those people who'd already convicted her in their minds—people from whom a pool of jurors would be selected.

Annie realized that Cole had resumed his seat and was watching her. "How do you like Denver?" she asked to fill the silence while they waited for his secretary to come back with the copies.

"It's a nice city," he said noncommittally. "The

winters took some getting used to, but it's home for me now. I've made friends. I've settled in.''

No mention of a wife or a family. All Annie could think to do was nod. The gap of six years yawned between them like a chasm with no bridge.

"What about you?" he asked unexpectedly. "I was surprised to hear you left the force. Being a cop meant so much to you."

Not as much as you did, she thought sadly. Even though she knew he was only making small talk, she considered her reply carefully. "It meant a great deal to my father that I followed in his footsteps," she said after a moment. "When I was cleared, I realized that being a cop had been his dream, but it was no longer mine." There was no way to explain how she'd felt, abandoned by Cole, ostracized by her fellow officers and gagged by the code of silence, the blue wall, from doing any more than declaring her own innocence. If her partner hadn't finally deigned to clear her of being on the take, Annie's career and her reputation would have been destroyed.

Because of her unwillingness to implicate her partner and Cole's subsequent lack of faith in her, he had assumed she was guilty. Perhaps it had been unrealistic of her to expect him to believe in her innocence without question, but, if the tables had been turned, she knew she would never have doubted him.

"I was sorry to hear about your father," he said

quietly, bringing her back to the present. "I thought about writing later, but it didn't seem like a good idea."

Annie didn't respond. What more was there to say? Instead she changed the subject. "I'll want to talk to your mother."

Instantly, his expression grew wary. "Why? She's already discussed this ad nauseam with the police, the prosecutor and with me. Is it necessary for you to drag her through it all again?"

"I like to do my own interviews." Annie struggled for patience. Was he going to oppose her every step of the way? What was he afraid of? "I may find something that's been overlooked."

"I can answer any questions you have," he insisted as his secretary slipped back in and handed him two sets of papers, one of which he gave Annie.

She knew from past experience that he could be bulldog stubborn when he wanted to be. She waited until the door closed again. "When did your mother notice the bracelet was missing?" she asked.

It was his turn to hesitate. Frowning, he referred to the file in front of him. "After a horseback ride at the ranch. It's all in here. She'd been having some trouble with the clasp. When she realized she'd lost the bracelet, she assumed it fell off somewhere out on the range, that it was gone forever."

"And did Ryan corroborate her story?" Annie persisted.

His frown deepened. "Ryan wasn't aware it was missing," he finally admitted.

"And why not?" It was important Annie put the pieces together, and the bracelet was the most damning piece of evidence the other side had.

Cole sat back in his chair and glared as though she were the enemy. "I don't know why not."

She got to her feet. "That's precisely why I need to talk to your mother. If someone did frame her, they had to have that bracelet with them at the time of the murder. How many people knew she was going to be at the hotel for the banquet?"

"I have no idea. Her room was comped and any number of hotel employees could have known." He pulled a calendar out of his drawer and flipped through it. "Let me call and set up a time for us to see her."

"No. Give me her number. *I'll* call her and *I'll* go talk to her." Annie refused to let him run her investigation. When he raked a hand through his black hair and she saw the worry in his eyes, she relented slightly. "I know what I'm doing," she said. "Let me do my job."

Cole appeared about to argue when his intercom buzzed. Muttering a soft curse, he picked up his phone. After a moment, he held it out to Annie. "It's Mom," he said, resignation in his voice. "She wants to see you."

"So you're the same Annie Jones my son used to know before he moved to Denver," Lily said just

as Annie was about to take a sip from the tall, sweat-
ing glass of iced tea brought by the housekeeper Lily
had introduced as Rosita.

The two women were sitting in the shade of the
inner courtyard at Ryan's sprawling ranch house,
surrounded by well-tended pots of flowering vines
and exotic grasses. Nearby a fountain gurgled softly.
The day was warm, but Lily's comment sent a sudden chill through Annie, and she set her glass down
abruptly.

"That's right," she replied, grateful her voice was
just as steady as Lily's gaze. "Cole and I were lovers six years ago. It ended badly." Perhaps her can-
dor would head off any more questions.

The older woman seemed to relax, as if she'd
been expecting evasion, even lies, and was relieved
to hear the truth.

"You don't have to tell me anything more," she
said as she selected a cookie from the silver tray.
Her engagement ring, studded with precious stones,
flashed a rainbow of colors in the sunlight. "I
haven't said anything about it to my son, but I
thought I remembered your name."

"You may have noticed some awkwardness between us," Annie replied without thinking. "I'm
sure Cole resents my presence as well as my involvement in this case." Now why had she added
that? His mother would naturally take his side if she
knew the details Annie had no intention of reveal-

ing. Heat climbed up her cheeks, heat that had nothing to do with the temperature of the air around them.

To her surprise, except for a flicker of satisfaction, Lily's expression remained pleasantly friendly as she bit into a delicate lemon wafer. Annie was relieved the older woman wasn't going to grill her. Taking the opportunity to change the subject, she opened the folder she'd brought with her and uncapped her pen. One by one, she dealt with the list of questions she'd jotted down earlier.

"You weren't wearing the ruby bracelet at the hotel?"

"No," Lily replied without hesitating. "I'd lost it before then."

"But you didn't tell Ryan. Why was that?"

"Because it was valuable, and I knew he'd want to replace it right away," Lily explained. "That's the way he is. I thought someone who knew it was mine might find it." Her smile wobbled around the edges. "I guess I was right."

Her explanation carried the ring of truth; Annie figured a jury might buy it. "How many people knew you were going to be at the Austin Arms that night, besides the staff?"

Lily thought for a moment. "I'm sure my name was mentioned in the advance publicity about the banquet," she recalled. "Anyone reading the newspaper could have known."

"Did you see anyone that night who might have

wanted to cause Sophia harm?'' Annie hoped that
Lily might remember something, anything, that
would give her a new lead.

Lily's smile was wry. "I'm sure the woman had
a few enemies, but I don't recall anyone in particular
other than the names I already gave the police. Do
you have a copy?''

Annie nodded. She had a list of everyone registered at the hotel that night, as well as the other
names the police had come up with.

"I told them a while ago Sophia had tried to bribe
me to stop seeing Ryan," Lily said. "When that
didn't work, she threatened me. I don't suppose telling them was the smartest thing to do.''

"Being honest is never a mistake," Annie told
her. "Especially if you're innocent.''

"You haven't made up your mind about that yet,
have you?'' Lily asked, smiling.

Annie surprised herself by smiling back. "I'm
working on it." She was beginning to like Cole's
mother. Despite her own words, she was starting to
question Lily's guilt.

She appeared physically fit enough to have committed the crime, but Annie doubted Lily had the
strength to overcome the other woman while re-
maining totally unscathed herself. Except for one
unexplained bruise on her upper arm, Lily hadn't
had any scratches or other injuries indicative of the
kind of fight suggested by the condition of the suite.

Thanking Lily for her time, Annie closed the

notebook. For now, her questions had been answered to her satisfaction. Lily had heard the rumors about Sophia's affairs, but she had no idea with whom the other woman had been involved.

As Annie took a healthy swallow of her iced tea, Lily suddenly snapped her fingers. "I just remembered something else," she blurted. "I don't know how I could have forgotten, but the way Sophia acted was just so hurtful to Ryan that I must have tried to put everything about her out of my mind." Her dark eyes sparkled with excitement.

"What is it?" Annie asked hopefully.

"This is third-hand gossip, at least," Lily said with a nervous laugh, "but you could check with Ryan for more details. He heard it from his niece, Eden."

"Heard what?" Annie prompted.

"Eden said that Sophia did have an argument with someone at the Austin Arms, where she was killed."

"The night of the murder?" Annie exclaimed, gaping. "And Eden witnessed it?"

"Wouldn't that have been convenient?" Lily asked. "No, it was a while ago, and Eden didn't actually see it. Her husband—well, they weren't married at the time—he was the one who was there. When the argument turned nasty, he became concerned for Sophia's safety, so he stepped in. From what he said, she didn't appreciate his interference. She turned on him like a shrew, demanding that he mind his own business. The whole scene must have been very unpleasant.''

Impatiently Annie waited for Lily to continue. Instead Lily plucked the fresh mint from her glass and sniffed it with obvious appreciation.

''Who was the man?'' Annie demanded.

''Eden's husband?'' Lily asked, blinking.

Annie struggled for patience. ''No, the man with Sophia.''

''Oh, I thought I told you.'' Lily dropped the mint back into her glass. ''It was Clint Lockhart. Ryan's first wife, Janine, was Clint's sister.''

''Do you think he and Sophia were involved?'' Annie asked. ''Is he attractive?''

Lily shivered delicately. ''I certainly don't think so, but there's no accounting for some people's taste. I guess you could say he was handsome in a very obvious way, though. I didn't know him well, but he had an arrogance about him that made me uncomfortable. As though he expected women to drop at his feet.''

In Annie's book, the man sounded like a possible suspect. ''I know the type.'' She made a note to call Eden. ''He doesn't work here anymore. Do you know why he left?''

Lily shrugged. ''I don't think Ryan ever mentioned it.''

''I wonder if the police questioned him,'' Annie muttered as she leafed through the file Cole had given her.

The housekeeper came out and asked if either of them wanted more iced tea. Annie declined absently.

"Thank you, Rosita," Lily replied. "The cookies were wonderful."

The older woman was grinning widely as she left. "She's worked here since she was fourteen," Lily remarked when Rosita was out of earshot. "And she claims to be psychic. Isn't that remarkable?"

"Uh-huh." Having found the appropriate statement, Annie read it in silence. Her shoulders slumped with disappointment. "Unfortunately, Clint Lockhart has what appears to be an airtight alibi," she told Lily. It didn't sound as though he could have killed Sophia, but he certainly had been involved with her in some way. He might know more than he'd told the police. Perhaps it would be worth Annie's time to check him out, after all.

"Do you think Ryan would have a snapshot of Lockhart I could borrow?" she asked.

Lily frowned. "Sure. There are a lot of family photos in the den. I'll get one on the way out. But why do you want a picture of Clint?"

"Call it a hunch." Shoving the papers back into her bag, she gave Lily a reassuring smile. "You've been a big help," she said. "I'll keep you posted."

"I appreciate anything you can do for my case," Lily replied, rising. "We're lucky to have you." Despite the shadow of worry in her eyes, her smile was warm. "I'll get you that photo and then I'll walk you to your car."

When they got to Annie's Volkswagen, she tucked the picture in her bag and promised to be in touch.

"Feel free to ask me anything," Lily insisted. "I think you and my son will make a great team. Are you seeing him again soon?"

"We're only working together on this one case," Annie pointed out quickly. "I'm not certain just when I'll be talking to him next, but rest assured that I'll keep him informed of any developments."

"Of course," Lily murmured.

"Cole told me he'd be going back to Denver as soon as the trial is over," Annie felt compelled to add, hoping she wasn't dashing the other woman's expectations that he would stick around.

"Texas has always been his real home," Lily insisted. "Maybe he'll change his mind about leaving."

Where Cole lived meant nothing to Annie, and she nearly said as much. Then she felt a pang of pity for the woman facing her with such a brave front. If she wanted to pretend her son might stay in Texas, who was Annie to disillusion her? "Wouldn't that be nice," she said.

"I'm glad you think so." Lily's tone was bland, her expression innocent. Surely, in the midst of everything else she was going through, she wouldn't be contemplating anything as ridiculous as a little matchmaking on the side, would she?

There was no way Annie could ask without looking like a complete fool. Frustrated, she bid Lily goodbye and climbed into her car. The interior was like an oven, the vinyl seat burning through the thin cotton of her slacks. At least the sudden discomfort was enough to distract her from the awkward and potentially humiliating idea of Cole's mother playing Cupid.

Considering the circumstances, that would have been a real recipe for disaster.

Three

"Hey, bro, working hard as usual?" Hannah Cassidy asked in a teasing voice from the doorway to Cole's borrowed office.

Cole looked up from his notes with a grin. He and his sister had always gotten along well. "How's the wedding business?" he asked.

Hannah owned a shop called The Perfect Occasion. "Business is slow," she replied. "I got tired of my own company, so I thought I'd come down and visit you."

"Bull," Cole responded mildly. "You came to check on your fiancé. All I am is a convenient cover story."

Hannah blushed, and Cole wondered why he had ever thought she was plain. Perhaps it was because next to their mother and youngest sister, with their dramatic coloring, Hannah had appeared merely pretty. Now he had to admit that love had transformed her. Her gray eyes shimmered with quiet happiness and her normally pale cheeks were flushed a soft pink. "I wanted to see you too," she protested. "You're my favorite brother."

"Your only brother," Cole pointed out dryly before he relented and got to his feet. "Come on in." He gave her a brief, hard hug. "How's Mom today? Have you talked to her?"

A shadow flickered across Hannah's face. "That's what I wanted to discuss with you. On top of everything else she's got to deal with right now, Mom's worried about Maria."

Cole clamped down on his annoyance. Their younger sister was as different from gentle Hannah as night from day. For as long as he could remember, Maria had been a huge pain—difficult, lazy and self-centered. Apparently it was too much to hope that for once in her life she'd put someone else's needs ahead of her own.

He shoved his hands in his pockets and rocked back on his heels. "What's our baby sister done now?"

Hannah closed the door behind her and took a seat, placing her leather purse in her lap. "Am I keeping you from your work?" she asked when she noticed the papers scattered across his desk.

Cole shook his head impatiently. "I'm just making a list of things for the investigator to look into." He'd paged Annie, but so far she hadn't responded. "Tell me about Maria."

Hannah folded her hands neatly on her purse. "Ever since she got back from California last year, she's been acting odd, even for her."

"How so?" Cole prompted.

"For one thing, she's always criticizing Ryan, insisting that he's just taking advantage of Mom and that he'll never marry her."

"Good grief," Cole exclaimed. "All men aren't like the jerks Maria hangs out with. Ryan adores Mom. What's Maria thinking?"

Hannah shrugged. "Mom hardly sees her, and then, when she does, Maria goes on about how Ryan will end up breaking Mom's heart."

Cole swallowed a curse. "From the beginning, she's been dead set against Mom and Ryan's relationship. Maybe she's jealous because our mother has found a good man who genuinely cares for her."

"Maybe," Hannah agreed. "Maria's so full of anger and resentment, as if Mom was the one with all the money and Ryan was some gold-digging bum, trying to take advantage of her. Mom's the one who broke up with him a long time ago and married Daddy instead."

Because she was pregnant with me, Cole thought, but he didn't say anything to his sister. When their mother was young, she'd listened to Ryan's brother's lies and been seduced by him, even though she was in love with Ryan. Afterward she was too ashamed to tell Ryan that she'd not only slept with his brother Cameron, but was carrying his child. That shame had kept the two of them apart for more than thirty years. Cole had grown up believing the man his mother married when she realized she was pregnant was his biological father. It had only been since Lily's arrest that she finally told Cole and Ryan the truth—that Chester Cassidy, who'd always loved Lily from afar, had agreed to marry her and pretend the baby was his. No one else knew yet, and Cole intended to keep it that way until after the murder case was resolved.

"All Ryan wants is for Mom to be cleared of these charges so they can get married," Cole told Hannah. "He'd marry her now if she'd agree, but you know how stubborn she is. Maybe Maria's biggest beef is that for once she's not the center of attention. She always wants to grab the spotlight away from anyone else."

A shadow of pain crossed Hannah's face. Maria had tried to ruin her happiness by coming on to her fiancé, Parker. Lucky for Maria that Hannah wasn't one to hold a grudge, even though she'd been deeply hurt by her sister's betrayal.

"Since she got back from California, she's gotten downright secretive," Hannah contradicted him with a frown. "She's practically forbidden us to visit her trailer without an engraved invitation. Mom's afraid she may be in some kind of trouble."

"What else is new?" Cole demanded. "Sounds to me like she's gotten mixed up with some man. That's Maria's usual style."

"But why would that make her act so strangely?" Hannah asked. "When she does come around, she's so tense you'd think she was going to snap, she's skinnier than ever and she looks worn-out. I almost feel sorry for her."

"That's pretty generous of you," Cole said.

Hannah shrugged. "Parker loves me. It's getting easier to forget what she tried to do." Absently, she fiddled with her engagement ring. "If Mom dares to ask Maria any questions, she throws a fit and accuses her of prying."

"Usually whenever Maria has a new man in tow, she can't wait to show him off," Cole commented. "I keep waiting for her to strap one of them to the hood of her car like a trophy deer."

Privately he wondered if resentment of Hannah's happiness had sent her over the edge. In school Hannah had been the quiet one, while Maria, all flash and flirt, had a line of men sniffing after her. Maria had liked nothing better than to rub her older, less popular sister's nose in her success with boys. But Parker was an attorney with a lucrative practice— attractive and athletic. Anyone with eyes could see that he adored Hannah. Maria had really misjudged him by thinking he'd respond to her advances.

Cole envied them their obvious devotion to each other. He hadn't felt that way about a woman since…since Annie Jones. The realization was a sobering one.

"Maybe Maria's gotten herself involved with a married man this time," he suggested. "One who insists on keeping a low profile."

Hannah's frown cleared. "You think it's something as simple as that? It sounds as though she's turned into a recluse down in Leather Bucket. She hardly comes to town at all.'' She let out a deep breath. ''Maybe you're right.''

''Have you tried talking to her?'' Cole asked. Despite Hannah's comment to the contrary, he knew her wedding consulting business kept her very busy. She and Parker had delayed their own ceremony until after Lily's trial, but she had other commitments. Parker had grumbled to Cole just the day before that Hannah put in longer hours than he did.

Hannah shook her head. ''I stopped by her place one day after an appointment, figuring it was time to smooth things over, but she wasn't home.'' There was a slight edge of resentment in Hannah's voice. She and Maria had never been close, even before Maria tried to steal Parker. But they were sisters, and Hannah had a forgiving nature. ''I just wish she'd quit worrying Mom and trying to put a damper on her happiness with Ryan. Mom has little enough to be happy about right now.''

Hannah glanced at her watch and got to her feet. ''Well, I have an appointment back at the shop,'' she said hastily. ''Sorry I unloaded on you when you're so busy.''

''Don't concern yourself,'' Cole said. ''I'll give Maria a call myself and see what I can find out. Meanwhile, Mom needs all our support until this mess is resolved. Just keep reminding her how much we all love her. I'm getting sick of our baby sister's selfishness."

"Thanks." Hannah hesitated in the doorway. "How's the investigation going? Any news?"

It wasn't the time to explain about Annie. "It's going fine," Cole replied. "The state's case appears to be full of holes. Establishing reasonable doubt should be easy." Not that he intended to go to court with anything that unreliable. Juries could be unpredictable, and there had been a lot of publicity. He wanted proof of their mother's innocence that no one could overlook.

"Mom couldn't have better representation," Hannah said loyally. "Will you tell Parker I said goodbye? He's in consultation until lunchtime."

Cole agreed, gave her a brotherly kiss on the cheek and watched her light step as she hurried from the office. He hoped the other attorney realized how lucky he was to have found her.

How could two sisters be so damn different? And how would Hannah deal with the news that Cole was only her half brother? He suspected he already knew what Maria's reaction would be—more fuel for her hatred of the Fortunes.

It was late when Annie locked the door to her office and headed for her car. The other shops were all closed and the parking lot was nearly deserted. Storm clouds had rolled in this afternoon, blotting out the sun and replacing its warmth with something heavy and cloying. Now even the darkness seemed to have an ominous substance.

Discouragement sat on her shoulders like dead weight. She'd spent the day interviewing employees of the Fortune empire she thought might know something about Sophia and Clint Lockhart, or the identity of the woman's most recent lover. Although the murdered woman hadn't been well liked, people were still reluctant to talk. Annie hadn't learned anything helpful. Back at her office, she had called Eden, who could add nothing helpful concerning the argument between Sophia and Clint Lockhart. She'd returned Cole's page, but he'd been unavailable. Then she had gone back over her notes, looking for something—however slight—that she might have missed before.

Glad the long day was over, she had just opened the door to her Volkswagen when another car drove into the small lot and pulled up beside her. Annie's gun was in her purse. Out of habit she checked to make sure the flap was unfastened as she squinted past the brightness of the headlights, trying to see the driver. The moment the lights blinked out, she recognized Cole behind the wheel.

Annie's weariness disappeared. Bracing herself, she waited for him to emerge from his fancy sedan. He was here on business; of that there was no doubt. The two of them didn't have a personal relationship, not anymore. So why was her heart thudding in her chest and that little knot of tension in her stomach twisting like a corkscrew?

"I'm glad I caught you," he said as he joined her on the pavement. His hair was mussed as if he'd been raking his fingers through it. He used to do that when he was distracted or frustrated. It made him look more approachable, less polished. "Have you found out anything about the identity of Sophia's lover?" he asked. Apparently he considered a simple greeting unnecessary.

Annie clutched her purse more tightly and stared up at him. It figured that the oppressive humidity didn't appear to affect him, despite his dark suit. Except for his disorderly hair and the shadow along his jaw, he managed to look irritatingly well groomed. The man was unreal.

In comparison, Annie felt as grimy and disheveled as if she'd spent the day working as a field hand. Absently she licked her bare lips. No doubt her face was shiny too. Her stomach chose that moment to emit a low growl not unlike an unfriendly dog.

She was *feeling* distinctly unfriendly. And hungry—she hadn't eaten since lunch.

"Hello to you too," she replied, annoyed. "You're beginning to sound like a broken record. Is that why you paged me?"

If Cole noticed her sarcasm, he chose to ignore it along with her question. "Have you had a chance to interview anyone on the list Mom and Ryan gave you?" he asked instead.

"How did you know about that?" Foolish question. Lily had probably mentioned it to him.

"We're supposed to be working on this case together," he pointed out, annoying her further because he was right. "Mom mentioned it, along with that argument Eden's husband witnessed, when I talked to her last night. I thought you might need some help. I can take half the names and talk to them tomorrow."

"Thanks, but I've already interviewed everyone," Annie said, managing to keep the smugness from her voice. "Including Eden and her husband."

His brows rose in apparent surprise, but all he said was, "Any leads?"

Annie's exhaustion returned and she lifted her hair off her sticky neck, wishing she hadn't left it loose. "Not really. Look, can we discuss this in the morning? It's been a long day and I want to go home. I'm tired and hungry."

As Cole glanced at his watch, something gold and heavy, he had the grace to look uncomfortable. "I didn't realize it was so late. I've been working too, and I never thought about the time. How about we go somewhere and grab a bite? You can bring me up to speed."

"I don't think so," Annie said quickly. The last thing she needed when her defenses were down was to spend time with *him*. "There's nothing to tell. Eden's husband Ben was the one who actually saw the quarrel. He never told Eden about the specifics until Sophia was killed. It didn't seem all that significant until then. The only thing Eden's husband had been able to add about Sophia's argument with Clint was how angry they both were, and then how quickly she leaped to his defense. Ben figured she was sleeping with him, but unless I can find a dent in Lockhart's alibi, none of that will matter.'' She rolled her shoulders to loosen them. "Maybe Sophia had moved on to someone else before she was killed. Either no one knows, or they don't want to tell me. As unpopular as Sophia was, I can't imagine why people would want to protect her.''

"Maybe they're afraid,'' Cole suggested.

"Of what? The woman's dead.''

His eyes narrowed. "Maybe it's not her they're protecting. Someone killed her—that's pretty scary. Clint Lockhart has been known to have a nasty temper. He could have threatened anyone who might put the finger on him.''

The possibility had already occurred to Annie. "I haven't been able to find out where he went yet or why he left, but I will,'' she said aloud. "It just won't be tonight. Besides, my cat's waiting to be fed.''

Cole stepped closer. "So we'll eat at your house.''

She was tempted to lean against his solid bulk for a few moments and draw strength from him, as she had so many times in the past. Instead she gave him the lethal stare that usually worked quite well on persistent men. "I beg your pardon?"

"Give me your address," Cole said, obviously unfazed by her show of hostility. "I'll pick up a pizza or some Chinese. You can go home and feed your cat, then we'll eat while we talk."

"We have nothing to talk about that can't wait." He wasn't going to invade her personal space. When this case was over, the only memories she wanted of him were impersonal ones. "I'll call you in the morning." She got into her car, but, before she could pull the door shut, he grabbed it.

"What are you afraid of?" he asked as he closed it gently and leaned down to gaze at her through the open window.

"Not a damn thing." Just myself, she thought as she stared down at his hand—so close—and resisted the ridiculous urge to cover it with her own.

"Prove it," he persisted. "Where do you live?"

For a moment she withstood his gaze, ignoring the intense blue of his eyes and the sweep of his lashes. Did he think she was scared to be alone with him, that she couldn't resist the great Cole Cassidy? Annoyed, she rattled off directions, knowing as she did that she'd fallen for one of the oldest tricks in the world—blatant manipulation.

With a faint grin, he straightened and gave the VW a pat. "What do you want to eat?" he asked as she started the engine.

"It's your party. You pick." Without giving him

time to reply, she shifted gears and roared off as quickly as her old bug would go.

By the time Cole had picked up a pizza and driven to the address Annie had given him, his gut was churning with impatience and annoyance—impatience that they were no closer to solving his mother's case; annoyance at himself for not being able to get his awareness of Annie under control.

It wasn't as if there could be anything between them. He'd blown that once and for all, so why didn't his libido get the message his common sense was sending? He usually had more pride than to go drooling after a woman who'd probably rather run him down with her rattletrap of a toy car than give him another chance.

Damn, but she'd looked good standing in the glow from his headlights, wearing a red-and-white striped top that hugged her breasts and the snug jeans she still favored. His blood flowed hot and fast as a memory of their lovemaking flashed through his mind—more vivid than any six-year-old image had a right to be. Cole was no monk and he'd been with a few women since Annie, but never had he felt the desire, the connection or the completeness he'd experienced with her.

Now he'd better get his feelings under control before her sharp eyes or her tracking skills zeroed in on his attraction to her. He needed her. His mother needed her. Whether or not she was the best private investigator around, as Ryan insisted she was, there wasn't time to start over with someone else. Besides, his mother liked Annie. She'd said so, several times. All Cole had to do was keep it professional between them. How hard could that be?

On top of everything else, the pizza was getting cold. Resolutely he climbed out of his car and headed up the well-lit steps of her town house.

As Cole shifted the pizza box and his keys so he could ring the bell, he glanced around at the neatly trimmed grass and the scattering of trees. The complex was a lot nicer than her old apartment building with its crumbling stucco and cracked roof tiles. There was no one around and, except for the sound of an occasional car on the nearby street, the area was remarkably quiet. Compared to his own busy apartment in Denver, this place was like a cemetery.

When the door opened, Cole braced himself for another battle. Annie's reluctance to talk to him tonight hadn't escaped him; he'd just ignored it. They had a lot of ground to cover before the trial.

"Come in." Her voice lacked enthusiasm as she stood aside, holding a cat the color of orange soda. As Cole walked by with the pizza, the creature's ears flattened and its glassy gold eyes never left him. Cole wondered what had ever happened to her old gray tabby.

"Does your cat like anchovies?" Cole asked.

Annie shut the door with a look of almost comical dismay. "You brought a pizza with anchovies?"

He remembered that she despised them, but he couldn't resist teasing her. She'd always been so gullible. "You don't care for them?" he asked, injecting as much surprise into his tone as he could manage.

"Never mind. I'm starving." Annie set the cat on the back of a plaid chair. She took the box from Cole and carried it over to the dining room table where she'd already set out plates, napkins and two woven placements. Nothing in the room was familiar to him. Her old place had come furnished, but she'd gussied it up with little extra knickknacks and doodads she was always picking up at thrift shops and garage sales. At the time he'd thought it too cluttered, but now he had to admit this cozy room was a whole lot more appealing than his own sterile apartment.

"Maybe Sluggo would eat the anchovies from my share," she muttered as she opened the box. For a moment she just stared and then she looked at him, her expression unreadable.

"What is it?" he asked, feeling a little silly for teasing her.

"You remembered." Annie's eyes were wide as she glanced at him and then away, as if she didn't know where to look.

Puzzled, Cole studied the pizza and then his face went hot. He felt awkward as hell. Without thinking, he'd ordered the same combination they'd always shared years before: ham with pineapple and black olives.

"I still like it," he said defensively, even though he hadn't eaten that particular combination since their breakup. He preferred pepperoni, and that was what he'd meant to order.

Annie was the first to recover. "This sure beats those nasty little fish," she remarked, gesturing for him to take a seat. "Do you want a soda or a beer?"

Cole shrugged out of his suit jacket and hung it on the back of the chair. "A beer sounds good."

When she went into the kitchen, he followed her curiously as he stripped off his tie. She opened the refrigerator, glancing over her shoulder.

"How long have you lived here?" he asked, dropping his cuff links into his pocket and rolling back his sleeves.

She'd done things with the kitchen too. A row of small copper pots filled with herbs sat on the windowsill. Apparently she still liked to cook with them. A collection of magnets, all cats, were scattered over the front of the fridge, which was white like the stove and the counters. A shallow basket filled with mail and papers rested next to a black-and-yellow cookie jar shaped like a bumblebee. Cole remembered the day she'd bought it.

The cabinets were whitewashed wood and the walls were covered with blue-and-white checkered paper. Ruffled curtains hung from the window over the sink—no sterile plastic blinds for her.

"I moved in about a year ago," she replied, leaning against the counter with a bottle of beer in each hand and a guarded expression on her face. "Why?"

Cole shrugged and took the beer from her. "Just curious. It seems like a nice complex."

She took two glasses from the cupboard. "It's quiet and it's not far from my office." She led the way back to the dining area. "Do I need to reheat the pizza?"

"Not unless you're a whole lot less hungry than I am," he drawled, pulling out a chair for her.

Annie sat down and served them each two slices while Cole poured their beer. The memories of other, more intimate evenings threatened to intrude on his mind and erode his composure. Times they'd eaten cold pizza in bed, or had it for breakfast the next morning because they never got around to it at all the night before.

He needed to forget the past and focus on the business between them. "I want to hear what progress you've made," he said around his first bite.

It took Annie a moment to switch back to professional mode. She'd been hoping he might say something more about her condo. When she'd bought the unit it had been white and impersonal, but she'd worked hard to make it a home. She'd put up wallpaper, sewed curtains and chair pads, stenciled borders, and searched for just the right accessories to give the place warmth and individuality. Had he forgotten the way they used to comb sales and second-hand stores, searching for items for her tiny apartment? Did he remember the decorating magazines she'd pored through or the day she'd found the cookie jar? Probably not.

His indifference to her efforts was disappointing. No doubt what she considered warm and cozy just looked messy to Cole, like her collection of Native American pottery in the living room, the pillows scattered on the couch or the candles she enjoyed burning. If memory served, his taste ran to chrome and leather. His kitchen counter was probably black granite. His borrowed office was devoid of personal touches. Even the carved jade cat was sleek and cold.

The smell of the pizza commanded her attention and made her mouth water. Before she told him who she'd talked to, she took a big bite and forced herself to chew it slowly while he watched with obvious impatience. Silently she demolished the entire slice, licking her fingers one by one before she picked up her beer. After she took a few sips, she leaned back in her chair and sighed.

"I needed that," she admitted, patting her stomach. "Thanks for bringing it."

"When did you eat last?" Cole growled. For a moment, familiarity shimmered between them like a ghost. When she'd been a rookie cop and he a young attorney, he'd nagged her all the time about skipping meals. They used to laugh about how he was always feeding her.

Appetite suddenly gone, she shoved her plate aside and reached for her bag. "I ate earlier," she said, pulling out her notes. "What I need now is to find Clint Lockhart. There are a few questions that want answers, and I think he's the one to give them to me."

Cole was regarding her over the rim of his glass. "Lockhart's not someone to fool with," he replied. "If he had anything to do with Sophia's death and he thinks you're after him, it could be very dangerous."

Annie shrugged and nibbled at a piece of ham she'd plucked off the pizza. She had to get some answers. Eliminating Lockhart as a suspect would help. "I can take care of myself. That's what I get paid for."

"We're *paying* you to help clear my mother, not get yourself killed," Cole snapped, voice rising. From the couch where he'd curled up, Sluggo lifted his head.

"Who said anything about getting killed?" Annie scoffed. "Lockhart was seen arguing with Sophia. They had a connection of some kind, and we probably know what it was. I want to make sure he wasn't still involved with her when she died."

"He has an alibi," Cole reminded her, putting aside his own plate and propping his elbows on the table. With his tie loosened and his sleeves rolled up, he looked devilishly attractive. "The police ruled Lockhart out as a suspect."

"But we haven't," Annie replied, flushing when she realized she'd included Cole in her statement. They weren't a team—not professionally and certainly not personally. She worked alone. "It's another piece of the puzzle."

"I want to be there when you question him." Cole's voice was flat, determined.

"No way," Annie exclaimed. "He'll clam up. I'll handle him myself."

Cole leaned forward, eyes narrowed. "And just how are you going to do this 'handling'?"

The thinly veiled insult sent Annie's temper soaring. Shoving back her chair, she got to her feet. "Just what gives you the right to question how I do my job? You aren't the one paying my fee."

For a moment, Cole looked furious. Then he got up too. Looming over her, he said in a low, intense voice, "I don't want you hurt. Is that so hard to understand?"

Annie stared as emotions she thought she'd dealt with bubbled up inside her. She'd never had the chance to confront him. But if he wanted a scene now, she would give him one. "You hurt me more than anyone else in my whole life." Her voice shook with raw feeling. "So you'll have to understand if I don't put a lot of faith in your concern."

Cole stepped back as if she'd slapped him and a muscle jumped in his cheek. "I'm sorry." His voice was a rasp. Instantly Annie regretted exposing herself the way she had. If only she could take back the impetuous words.

"Forget it." She grabbed their dirty plates and headed for the kitchen, assuming he was no more interested in eating the cooling pizza than she was. She didn't know he'd followed her until she heard him whisper her name. Setting down the dishes, she kept her back to him.

"I'd like you to leave." She held her voice steady through sheer force of will.

"Annie," he said again, cupping her shoulders with his hands. "Look at me."

She stiffened, chin up, willing it not to wobble. Finally he let her go. He'd always liked to touch, she remembered—holding her hand, lacing fingers with hers, stroking her cheek, draping an arm across her shoulders. He'd said he liked feeling the connection. Now her eyes filled with tears that she blinked fiercely away.

When he'd left her, pride had been the only thing stopping her from begging him to believe in her. When she'd been cleared of all charges, it was pride that kept her from contacting him with the proof of her innocence. And when she quit the force, scared to death of striking out on her own but determined to succeed, pride had refused to let her give up.

Well, that same stubborn pride damn well wasn't going to let her down now.

Swallowing, she turned and gave him a steady,

dry-eyed stare. She refused to tremble or to show the slightest sign of weakness. "I asked you to leave. This was a mistake. We'll have to discuss the case at my office during work hours."

Cole started to speak and then he must have seen her determination. Sighing, he speared his fingers through his hair. The familiar gesture was nearly Annie's undoing.

"This isn't over," he said as he spun on his heel and grabbed his jacket from the dining room chair.

"This is *my* investigation," she felt compelled to remind him as he headed for the door. "As Lily's attorney, you have a right to be kept informed, but you're not going to order me around or tell me how to do my job."

Cole hesitated, his hand on the knob. "Then you damn well better come up with something soon. You're supposed to be a real hotshot P.I. It's time you proved it."

As Annie sputtered furiously, trying to come up with a suitable retort, he yanked open the door and went out, pulling it closed behind him. The *click* of the latch echoed in the sudden silence of her town house like a gunshot.

Four

The moment Cole shut the door behind him, he felt a stab of regret. Annie's words, telling him how much he'd hurt her, echoed in his head. Too bad he couldn't go back and talk to her, but he had no idea how to make things better between them. It was years too late for that.

Resolutely he headed toward his car. She was the one who'd thrown him out, he reminded himself with a righteous little twitch of his shoulders. He couldn't go back if he wanted to. She was in no mood to listen, and he had no idea what to say if she was. Tell her again that he was sorry? That he regretted letting her down? That he wanted a second chance?

Cole climbed behind the wheel. Where the hell had that idea come from? Annie was a different person from the one who had loved him so unconditionally; she was a lot tougher now and more independent. He was the last thing she needed.

He had changed too. Except for his mother, there was nothing for Cole in San Antonio, not anymore. His life was in Denver.

Driving out of the tree-lined parking lot, he re-sisted the urge to examine that life too closely. De-spite the promise of a partnership in the near future at his law firm, he'd been feeling restless lately. That had to be normal considering everything that had happened—his mother's arrest for murder, followed by her confession that Ryan's late brother Cameron was his real father. Hell, anyone would feel a little disoriented after being hit with all that.

Besides, he reasoned as he glanced down at the speedometer and eased his foot off the gas, before he and Annie had broken up, he'd begged her to defend herself against those charges and to give him some kind of explanation he could understand, but she had refused. How was he supposed to have known she really was innocent? He wasn't psychic, after all!

Feeling justified, Cole kept his speed well under the limit as he headed toward Ryan's ranch. Half-way there, the storm that had been threatening all day finally broke over his car, pummeling his wind-shield with raindrops as fat and squishy as caterpil-lars. Explosions of thunder crashed around him and lightning filled the sky.

Damn the man! Hands shaking with reaction, An-nie poured hot water over a tea bag in one of her favorite cat mugs and forced herself to take several deep, calming breaths. The rumble of thunder that rattled the windows and sent Sluggo slinking up the

stairs to the relative safety beneath her bed seemed
like a fitting conclusion to the scene that had just
taken place in her living room.

Where had Annie lost control of the situation with
Cole? When he'd disparaged her abilities? When
he'd pretended to be oh, so concerned for her safety?
Or when *she* had blurted out how devastated she'd
been by their breakup?

Old, invulnerable Annie had finally let down her
guard and exposed her weakness—that was what really had her bugged. Tears filled her eyes and spilled
down her cheeks. Not to mention the fact that he'd
actually left when she told him to. Damn it, she
wanted him to argue, to fight, to hang on when she
pushed him away.

Juggling her mug of tea, Annie swiped at her wet
cheeks. She hated for him to know how much he'd
wounded her, how much his betrayal *still* hurt. And
she hated seeing how easily he left—just as he had
when he'd moved to Denver and started a new life,
as though what they'd created together didn't even
matter.

Lightning flashed and rain beat against the windows as she sipped the tea, burning her tongue. She
hoped Cole's pricy sedan had a leak in the roof and
that his fancy suit would get soaked in the down-
pour.

Well, maybe she couldn't take back her impulsive
confession, but at least she could do something
about finding Clint Lockhart. First thing tomorrow

she was going back to the Double Crown to question one of the ranch hands again. He'd seemed nervous when she first talked to him, making her suspect that he knew more than he was letting on. Someone had to have heard where Lockhart went after he quit the Double Crown without notice and dropped out of sight.

That settled, Annie curled up on the couch and reached for the TV remote. Perhaps, if the storm hadn't knocked out the cable, there would be a movie on that would lull her jangled nerves so she could get some sleep. She'd barely gotten comfortable when Sluggo came back down the stairs and jumped up next to her, looking for reassurance. Annie stroked his wide head and listened to his ragged purring.

At least there was one male in her life she could count on for unconditional affection. She'd be smart to remember that.

Her mind wandered as she watched the movie, a badly plotted thriller about a woman being stalked by a psycho. Since the heroine persisted in taking foolish chances despite several close calls and numerous warnings by the police, it was difficult to sympathize when she was nearly killed walking alone down a dark, deserted alley.

With a murmur of impatience, Annie turned off the television. In the blessed silence that followed, she mentally reviewed her conversation with the ranch hand she wanted to question again. Although

she was sure she'd never seen the man before, something about him seemed familiar.

She'd dug out her notes and was going back over
the police report when his name, Don Flynn, jumped
out at her. What a coincidence! Lockhart and Flynn
had been bunkhouse roommates. Yet he hadn't seen
fit to mention that to her, not even when she asked
how well he knew Lockhart.

According to the report, Lockhart had gotten a
phone call the night of the murder. The cowboy
who'd knocked on his door to get him told the police later that Lockhart had refused to take the call,
claiming he was too tired to get up. The other man
didn't remember what time the call came in, and he
hadn't actually seen Lockhart. Flynn was the one
who volunteered that he woke up and looked at his
clock, corroborating Lockhart's alibi.

So why was Annie reluctant to eliminate him as
a suspect? She reread Flynn's statement, checking
for loopholes. Several other bunkhouse residents remembered seeing Lockhart in the common room
earlier, but none of them could say for sure when
he'd gone to bed.

Annie rubbed her tired eyes. What wasn't she seeing?

The last voice Cole expected to hear through the
open doorway of Ryan's office at the ranch house
early the next morning was Annie's. For a brief mo-

ment, he wondered if she'd come to apologize for tossing him out. Then he caught her words.

"I want to talk to him again," she was telling Ryan. "He's scared, and I think he's hiding something."

As Cole hovered in the hallway, Ryan came out of the office with Annie. They both stopped when they saw Cole.

"What are you doing here?" she asked, obviously surprised. She was wearing jeans and a bright yellow T-shirt, with her hair in its usual ponytail. Earrings shaped like pineapples danced from her ears.

"Cole's staying with us," Ryan explained. "It made more sense than for him to take a room in town, and it's especially nice for Lily to have him around."

"Of course," Annie murmured, her gaze avoiding Cole's.

"I hope you aren't here to question Mom again," he said. "I don't think there's anything more she could add to what she's already told you."

"Don't forget that Annie's on our side," Ryan chided. "She's here for a follow-up with one of the ranch hands, but I was trying to persuade her to join me for coffee first."

Annie glanced from Ryan to Cole, her smile fading. "And I was telling Ryan that I'm under a great deal of pressure to find a new lead," she said sweetly. "In spite of the fact that my investigative methods have been called into question."

It was Ryan's turn to look from one to the other of them with obvious puzzlement. "Not by me," he said staunchly. "I have great faith in your abilities."

"Thank you." Annie looked as though she already regretted her outburst.

"Who's been pressuring you?" Ryan demanded. "Not Lily. She understands that unearthing the truth takes time."

"Oh, no," Annie said quickly. "Lily has been very cooperative." She gave Cole a haughty look and pressed her lips together.

"I think it's me Annie's referring to," he admitted. "We had a little misunderstanding last night that we need to clear up."

"Problems with the case?" Ryan asked.

"Among other things." Cole would be damned if he'd go into detail, especially with Annie glowering at him. "Nothing we can't work out, though."

"Perhaps the two of you would like to use my office," Ryan suggested, stepping aside. "I'll have Rosita bring you some coffee."

"Coffee won't be necessary, thanks," Annie said. "This will only take a moment. I want to catch up with Flynn."

"I'll be waiting to take you to him," Ryan said, and then he excused himself. As soon as he left, Cole followed Annie into the office, shutting the door and leaning his shoulder against it.

She whirled to face him, arms folded across her

chest. "I can't take time to talk now," she said impatiently. "I don't want to keep Ryan waiting."

"Would you just listen to me?" Cole asked, blocking her attempt to reach for the knob. He extended his hand in a conciliatory gesture, but she avoided his touch. Getting along together didn't seem to be an option.

"What do you want?" Her voice was edged with impatience and her eyes were dark with some emotion he couldn't read.

For his mother's sake, Cole tried again. "I'm sorry for some of the things I said last night." It surprised him how easily the words came out once he started. "I didn't mean to be so critical. You're doing a good job on this case and I admire your thoroughness." He jammed his hands into his pockets. "That's all."

For a moment Annie just looked at him while he tried to figure out what else to say. Then she relaxed her stance. "Okay," she said on a huff of expelled air. "Apology accepted."

"Would you mind explaining to me what you're going to do next?" Cole asked carefully. "I thought you already questioned the ranch employees. Who's this Flynn character?"

Briefly Annie filled him in. "He's holding back," she concluded. "I think something, or someone, has got him scared to talk."

Rocking on his heels, Cole studied her. With those silly pineapple earrings she didn't look so tough, but he felt as though he were picking his way across a minefield just the same. "Fear could make Flynn dangerous."

"The man's ready to bolt at his own shadow," Annie scoffed. "He doesn't worry me."

She still got to him, Cole realized with dismay. As if it were yesterday when he'd last held her, kissed her, he could remember her taste and the way her mouth softened under his. Damn!

"Whoever's scaring Flynn should worry you some," he said roughly, and then he realized he was doing it again. He eased back a notch. "Just be careful. I'd hate to have to find another P.I. at this point."

Her laugh stabbed him like a small, sharp knife. "I'm always careful."

Was her voice a shade huskier than usual? He wasn't sure. He just knew he'd better get out of Ryan's office before he did something guaranteed to shatter the tentative truce they seemed to have forged. Opening the door, he stepped back to let her by. When she looked up, her expression had lost some of its hostility.

"I'll keep you posted," she offered, and then she hurried away, leaving him to speculate as to whether it was possible that he bothered her anywhere near as much as she did him.

He was still working on that puzzle when he joined his mother for breakfast in the small sunroom. The way her face lit up made him feel guilty for the resentment he was still struggling with. Why couldn't he put his feelings aside? At the time she had done what she thought was best. He didn't have to agree with her to accept her motives.

"Good morning, darling," she exclaimed. "How did you sleep?"

What if, despite his best efforts, his mother was convicted? He shuddered to think of her in a prison cell. She was too vibrant for confinement, bubbling over with happiness now that she and Ryan had found each other again.

If Cole's efforts failed, he would always wonder if his personal feelings had held him back or clouded his judgment in some way. Dammit, he had to clear her!

"I slept well. How about you?" He leaned down to kiss her cheek. When he straightened, she searched his face as if she was looking for an answer to some unspoken question.

"What is it they say? I'm doing as well as can be expected, I guess." Her smile was brave, but there were dark smudges beneath her eyes. "Have you talked to Annie?" she asked. "Is there any progress?"

Cole pulled back the chair next to hers and sat down. "I just saw her. She was going to talk to one of Ryan's employees." He reached for the coffee carafe and topped off her cup before filling one for himself.

"Annie will find something," his mother said

with forced confidence. She speared a chunk of melon with her fork, but then she merely pushed it around her plate.

"You aren't eating enough," he admonished her. Was it his destiny to make sure the women in his life got fed?

She laughed softly. "Have you been talking to Ryan?" she teased. "The two of you seem determined to fatten me up." She glanced at the empty spot on the table in front of him. "What about you? Have some breakfast."

He shrugged. "Just coffee for me. I'll get something later." He would never tell her that grim image of her looking out from behind bars had destroyed his appetite. "Any news on the kidnapping?" he asked.

Her smile faded, and he wished he'd kept his mouth shut. "No, nothing." A note demanding several million dollars' ransom had shown up on the one-year anniversary of Ryan's grandson Bryan Fortune's disappearance, but no one had tried to pick up the money. Shortly after the baby had been kidnapped, the FBI recovered another male baby bearing the unique Fortune birthmark, the same mark Cole himself wore. No one knew where this child had come from, but since they knew he was a Fortune, all the Fortune males were tested for paternity. The test proved Matthew was his father. Matthew had claimed he never cheated on his wife Claudia, saying the only way he could be the father was from a sperm bank donation years ago. Lately the Fortune family had had more than their share of devastating luck.

"How do you like working with Annie?" his mother asked, breaking into his grim thoughts.

"She's competent enough," he replied cautiously.

Lily sipped her coffee. "She's pretty."

"I hadn't noticed."

For the first time in way too long, his mother laughed out loud. As Cole's cheeks flamed, she patted his hand. "Perhaps you've been working too hard," she suggested with mischief in her eyes.

"Annie Jones isn't my type," he grumbled.

"Since when?" she asked.

Would she remember Annie's name after all these years? "Since I've been working on an important case," he reminded her, growing more uncomfortable.

She looked at him with a thoughtful expression. "I guess I can't complain about that."

"Seen Maria lately?" Cole asked to change the subject. The ruse worked almost too well. Her smile faded.

"I'm worried about that girl," she said.

It was Cole's turn to laugh, even if it was without humor. "What else is new?"

The only good thing that had come out of her trip to the ranch that morning had been Cole's apology,

Annie fumed as she drove back to San Antonio. When she talked to Flynn, he had seemed even more nervous than before. Maybe she was wasting her time looking for Lockhart—she'd sure as heck wasted a couple of hours today.

Someone had been intimately involved with Sophia before her murder, though. Ryan's divorce attorney, Parker, had told Annie that he suspected Sophia of being in contact with someone at the ranch who was passing on information about Ryan's activities and his affair with Lily to help Sophia wring a bigger settlement from him.

A family member? Parker hadn't thought so, and neither did Annie. An embittered employee or one susceptible to a bribe was more likely, or one who liked sharing Sophia's bed.

The more Annie found out about the kind of person Ryan's second wife had been, the more she suspected that Lily wasn't the only one with a reason to kill her.

The next day, after Annie got back from Austin where she'd been talking to hotel employees, she finally got a break.

There was a message from Lily on her machine at home. Rosita had overheard one of the maids, who'd apparently been involved with and then dumped by Lockhart, mention that he'd gone to work at a dude ranch in the Hill Country. Before he'd left the Double Crown, he bragged about a lady friend who was in line for a big payoff of some kind. A divorce settlement?

Elated, Annie flipped open the *Yellow Pages* and started making calls. On her third try, she got lucky. The front desk confirmed that Lockhart was employed at a small family guest ranch called the Circle A. Now all she had to do was devise a cover story and drive there to check him out.

After she finished her second call to the ranch, disguising her voice, there was a knock on her door. She was in no mood for company; the information she had gotten about accommodations at the dude ranch only complicated the situation. She needed a whole new game plan.

Reluctantly she opened the door to find Cole on her front step holding two white paper sacks. He looked tired, as if the case against his mother was beginning to extract a toll. In place of his usual suit and tie, he was wearing jeans and a blue plaid Western shirt with pearl snaps. On his feet were scuffed cowboy boots. The casual attire made him appear less intimidating and even more attractive than usual.

"I brought Chinese this time," he said, extending the sacks like a peace offering. Instead of his rented Lexus, a blue pickup with the Double Crown logo on the side was parked at the curb.

Annie didn't have the energy to argue. She opened the door wider and gestured for him to come in.

"Been out busting horses and roping dogies?" she teased as she shut the door, trying to ignore the elemental feminine response that sizzled along her nerve endings. What was it about a cowboy, even a pretend one, that made a woman's heart beat faster?

For a moment Cole looked puzzled by her comment. Then he glanced down at himself and his frown cleared. "I had to get some of Mom's stuff out of storage to take to the ranch. I figured you might not have bothered to eat, so here I am."

Annie considered pointing out that she didn't like uninvited company, but she decided not to antagonize him when he'd brought food. "I was going to fix myself an omelette," she said. It wasn't really a lie; she would have thought of eating eventually. "But you might as well stay. Actually, there are a couple of things I need to run by you."

Cole put the bags on the table, so she grabbed plates and forks from the kitchen. While he opened the cartons, releasing their wonderful aromas, she took a bottle of pear wine from the refrigerator and filled two glasses.

"What did you want to tell me?" Cole asked as they heaped their plates with almond chicken, sweet-and-sour pork, egg rolls and fried rice.

"I went to Austin today. No one I talked to at the hotel can remember seeing your mother wearing that ruby bracelet that was found in Sophia's suite, nor can they place her anywhere near there, as you know. Lily's room was on a different floor. I showed around a picture of Lockhart that your mother loaned me, hoping to find someone who remembered him, but I struck out. I guess that would have been too easy. Of course that doesn't mean he or someone else couldn't have slipped in and out. The hotel was busy that evening. I don't think the police searched very hard once they linked Lily with the bracelet. Unfortunately that can happen.''

Cole tipped his head to one side and gave Annie a challenging look. ''Still think she might be guilty?''

Slowly she shook her head. ''There are too many loopholes for me to assume that. Someone could have found the bracelet and either left it there deliberately or dropped it during the struggle. I'd like to tell her myself that I believe her, though.''

''Fair enough,'' he agreed. ''She'll appreciate hearing it. I'd like to go into court with something stronger than just the gaps in the state's case, so where do we go from here?''

''Actually I've located Lockhart's whereabouts,'' she said smugly, taking a bite of egg roll.

''No kidding! Are you going to talk to him?'' When she didn't immediately answer, Cole's grin was replaced with an expression of anxiety. ''What's wrong? He's not dead, is he?''

''Oh, no,'' Annie replied hastily. ''At least, not as of a few hours ago. Thanks to a tip from Rosita that your mother passed on to me, I found the guest ranch where he works. Of course I can't just confront him. If he's got something to hide, he'll clam up and disappear again." She stabbed a piece of almond chicken with her fork.

Naturally, Cole was using the chopsticks that had come with the dinner. Now he set them carefully on the edge of his plate and sat back in his chair. Being the recipient of his full attention was unnerving. "What are you telling me?" he asked softly.

"I'm going to visit the ranch," she said. "I need to search his room. Maybe I can find something incriminating."

For a moment, Cole merely stared as a flush ran up his lean cheeks. "Are you nuts?" he demanded. "We know Lockhart's got a temper. He may already have killed one woman. He could do it again. Even if he's not guilty, he might not like you pawing through his stuff."

"Give me a little credit," Annie retorted. "He's not going to catch me. Besides, I won't be going alone."

Cole shoved back his chair and got to his feet. "You're taking backup?" he asked, pacing.

"I guess you could say that." Annie wasn't sure why she didn't shut up right there. "The Circle A is a small, family-owned guest ranch." She felt some stupid compulsion to explain. "They're booked solid for weeks except for one cancellation, and they don't allow unmarried couples to room together."

The expression on Cole's face was almost comical. "Say again?"

Rolling her eyes, Annie repeated what she'd been told on the phone earlier. "They accept families and married couples in their guest cabins. Singles are welcome to stay in one of the bunkhouse dorms. Unfortunately, the women's dorm is full."

"The women's dorm?" Cole echoed. "Are you pulling my leg?"

How she wished she were. Under other circumstances, the situation might be humorous. "Unfortunately, I'm just repeating what a sweet-voiced older woman told me on the phone. And the only vacancy is the honeymoon suite."

Cole's expression turned dark and forbidding. "Get to the part about not going alone."

She shrugged. "I'm planning to ask another investigator to pose as my husband."

Cole muttered something she didn't understand, which from his expression was probably for the best. "How well do you know this other investigator?"

She shrugged. "He's a business acquaintance. We've worked together on a couple of cases."

"And you're willing to share a room with him? Isn't that carrying 'under cover' a little too far?" Cole demanded. His hands were bunched at his sides. If Annie didn't know better, she might think he was jealous.

Instead of asking, she retorted, "It's that way or no way." Looking up into his brooding face, she remembered with dismay how attractive she'd always found him to be when he was in a temper. Hastily she scrambled to her feet so she didn't feel quite so intimidated by his greater height.

"So you barely know this other guy?" he asked. "The one you don't mind staying with?"

It was Annie's turn to blush. "I resent your implication. This is business." Why was she explaining herself to Cole? "Besides," she added belatedly, "I have no choice."

"You don't need him," Cole said stubbornly.

"Yes, I do." Annie threw up her hands. "I already explained—"

"I'll go with you."

Share a room with *Cole?* He had to be crazy. "No way."

"Why not?" he asked. "You need a husband for a couple of days, right? I'm volunteering." His smile was devoid of humor. "At least you know I don't snore."

"It's out of the question." To be trapped together in the honeymoon suite? She refused to consider it. Frantically she cast around for a plausible excuse that wouldn't reveal her panic. "Robert's a trained investigator," she said. "You don't know how to use a gun."

He gave a shout of laughter. "Honey, I grew up in Texas. Think again."

"There's no way it would work," she insisted. Considering the begrudging attraction she still felt toward him, being in such close quarters together would be inviting trouble. She turned away. "No."

He grabbed her arm and spun her back around. "Yes," he said, looking determined. "If you're taking on a man like Lockhart, I want to be there." She shook her head and his hand tightened. "Don't fight me on this, Annie. You won't win."

The sudden inexplicable desire to give in, to melt against his strength and feel his arms around her, was far from her usual reaction to a bossy man, and she resented her own weakness. God help her, she would never be able to maintain her cool if he guessed her feelings. She struggled against his hold. "After all we've been through, I can't believe you'd think I'd even consider taking you with me."

"Why not?" he demanded. "You're apparently willing to go with some guy you hardly know."

"That's different," she cried. "Robert and I never—"

"Never slept together?" he cut in. "Is that what this is about? You think if we share a room I'll just naturally assume—"

It was Annie's turn to interrupt. "Of course not." She squeezed her eyes shut. He was so close that she could feel the heat radiating from his big body, smell his cologne and the underlying male scent she'd once loved. *Loved!*

"Then what is it?" he asked, voice softening. "Tell me."

She stared up at him, struggling for an answer he

would accept. Then something changed between them, the very air becoming charged with awareness. His gaze shifted to her mouth. His eyes narrowed.

"I think it's time we got something out of the way," he murmured, eyes darkening from blue to nearly black. "Maybe then we can move on without any distractions."

As soon as Annie realized what he had in mind, she froze. She wanted this, had wanted it since she'd first seen Cole again in that restaurant.

When he dipped his head, she lifted hers and met him halfway. The kiss was anything but tentative. Vaguely aware that his hands had shifted to her back, pressing her closer, Annie twined her arms around his neck and gave herself up to the sheer needy hunger bubbling through her.

The kiss was hot and wet and, oh, so welcome. Her mouth fused with his as heat exploded between them, and she would have sworn, had she been able to form words, that they shared a heartbeat. For a moment stolen out of time, Cole was the only thing in Annie's universe.

Five

Cole would have gone on kissing Annie until the building fell down around him, if he hadn't eventually realized through the red haze threatening to envelop him that she was trying to push him away. He'd never forced a woman and he never would, no matter how sweet she tasted. No matter how convinced he was that she wanted the kiss as much as he did.

Head swimming, heart thudding in his ears like a drum, he managed to snag the shreds of his control and lift his mouth from hers. He'd meant to show them both it was time to quit letting the past get between them. All he'd shown *himself* was that his attraction for Annie was very much in the present, and that sooner or later he was going to have to deal with it.

Annie's chest heaved as though she couldn't get enough air. Her lips were swollen and wet, her eyes clouded. All Cole wanted was to bury himself deep inside her while the little cries he remembered so well echoed in his ears.

"This was a mistake," she said, her words like a dash of cold water.

He wanted to tell her that no mistake had ever felt so right, and to ask if she always made them with so much enthusiasm. She'd been a full partner in that kiss.

"A mistake?" He didn't bother to keep the disbelief out of his voice. Damn it, she was retreating again. He dragged in a breath and rubbed a hand over his face, trying to collect his scattered thoughts. It hurt like hell that she hadn't been as affected— make that *stunned*—by the kiss as he had. "Yeah, I guess you're right." What else could he say when she was looking at him with such obvious regret, as though she'd just realized she'd been kissing a frog and not Prince Charming?

Annie's head was reeling, her lungs still struggling for oxygen. Her lips tingled and her arms felt suddenly empty. Her body burned where she'd plastered it against Cole's. Her overwhelming response to him brought with it a sense of panic. What if she hadn't put on the brakes, and he'd ended up prying her off him like a lovesick groupie? The image made her shudder with humiliation. How many times did the man have to walk away for her to get the picture?

He might like kissing her, but he didn't really want her. Not then and not now.

"We need to forget this ever happened," she said,

her knees giving out. She sank into a chair without looking at him.

"Shouldn't be too hard." His voice was steady, emotionless, making her wonder if he'd been affected at all. "It was only a kiss. I just figured we needed to get past it."

His male logic made her want to scream. "Yeah, whatever," she managed. Brilliant. Did she want him to see how deeply he could still affect her, to know she felt as though she'd been ripped apart and shoved back together in a totally haphazard way?

Annie struggled to find her footing. She even managed to flash him a rueful smile, though it felt so brittle she was afraid her whole face might shatter.

"So where were we?" she asked, taking what tiny, perverse satisfaction she could in his frown. Had he thought she'd make a scene? Slobber all over him like some pathetic Saint Bernard?

"I was objecting to your plan to take some P.I. you barely know with you to check out Lockhart."

"And I was trying to figure out what your problem is," Annie countered. Perhaps she should have been impressed by Cole's ability to switch back to work mode so effortlessly, but instead his dogged stubbornness just irritated her. "Lockhart's the best lead we have right now. If I have to pretend I'm married in order to get close enough to investigate the slimeball, that's what I'm going to do."

Cole folded his arms across his chest. "Fine, but I'm playing the part of your temporary husband."

"Why?" Annie huffed. He'd just proven he didn't care enough about her to be jealous, so what was his objection? "If you still don't think I can do the job—" she began hotly.

Cole held up a hand. "I already told you that I respect your abilities." He spun away, looked out the window. The set of his shoulders, rigid beneath his casual shirt, radiated tension. "She's my mother," he said softly. "I can't sit on the sidelines twiddling my thumbs while you save her. I need to take an active part in this investigation."

"The state's case is a joke," Annie argued. "I know you're worried, but there's plenty of room for reasonable doubt. You'll do your part in the courtroom."

"That's not good enough. I can't take any chances," he argued.

"It's not a matter of taking chances," Annie said. "It's me doing my job and you doing yours."

Cole's hand went to the back of his neck. Annie would have liked to ease some of that tension from his muscles, but he wouldn't appreciate her gesture. And she didn't dare touch him. "There's more to this than just doing my job," he said over his shoulder. "My relationship with Mom has been strained lately. If this goes wrong, I need to know I've done everything I could. I need for *her* to know that."

Annie tried her best to reassure him. "I'm sure

she does. You dropped everything back in Denver when you came here to defend her. That says a lot.''

Cole remained silent.

''I remember how you used to talk about her in such a loving way,'' Annie continued. ''You were so close. What's happened to change that? Surely not her relationship with Ryan? You wouldn't begrudge her that happiness, would you?''

With a sigh he turned to face her, his gaze intense. ''Of course not. It isn't Ryan who's the problem, it's my father—or at least the man I thought was my father.''

Annie was puzzled. Cole had always claimed that his parents' marriage had been a happy one. ''What are you saying?''

Cole sat down across from her, his hands clasped loosely between his bent knees. ''Mom was pregnant when she and my—when she and Chester got married.''

''Lots of people start out that way,'' Annie said, and then the gist of what he meant dawned on her. ''She was pregnant by someone else? Is *Ryan* your real father?'' It made sense. Ryan had told Annie that he and Lily were in love before she broke up with him and married Chester Cassidy.

''I wish it were Ryan,'' Cole replied. ''Maybe that would be easier to accept.''

Sluggo chose that moment to jump up on Annie's lap. Absently she stroked his fur. ''You don't have to tell me who it was,'' she said to Cole, sensing his reluctance. His parentage was really none of her business, and she wasn't sure how it tied in with her trip to the guest ranch, anyway.

"I *want* to tell you." He managed a fleeting grin that left his face even more bleak when it faded. "Mom hasn't told anyone except Ryan and me. We don't want my sisters to have to deal with it until this other business is resolved."

It was plain to see he was still having trouble accepting the news. What would it be like to find out after all this time that the man who'd raised you wasn't who you thought he was? She pictured her own father, so proud of her when she had joined the force and so devastated when she'd been painted as a dirty cop. Still, he'd stuck by her—the only one who had.

Perhaps she should stop Cole from saying any more, but she was curious. Although she'd never met the man who raised him, Cole had mentioned him often. They'd been close. "It must have been difficult for you," she murmured. "Is your biological father still alive? Have you met him?"

"He died a while back, but I knew who he was. It was Cameron Fortune, Ryan's brother."

Annie's face must have shown her shock. When he was alive, Cameron Fortune had earned himself a reputation as a playboy and a womanizer whose exploits, even during his marriage, were often featured in cheap exposés and gossip rags. "How did your mother ever get hooked up with a man like him?'' she blurted without thinking.

Cole didn't appear offended by her outburst as he stretched out his long legs and crossed his booted feet at the ankles. ''I certainly don't blame her for what happened,'' he said, ''but I don't know if she believes that. She didn't try to make excuses for her behavior, but Ryan told me a little more later. It seems that when he and his brother were growing up, Cameron always enjoyed tormenting Ryan. It would have been in character for Cameron to go after Lily once he found out that Ryan cared about her.''

Cole's face reflected his mixed emotions. How difficult this must be for him. ''Mom worked for Rosita in the kitchen. She didn't realize until it was too late that Cameron was only using her, playing on her insecurities to drive a wedge between her and Ryan. Once my father got what he wanted, he dropped her.''

''What an awful man,'' Annie exclaimed, forgetting for a moment his relationship to Cole. ''I guess I can understand why Ryan didn't want her either, after that.''

''Ryan didn't know about Cameron,'' Cole said, surprising her. ''Mom never told him. From what I've heard, I'm surprised Cameron didn't brag about it. I guess it was enough for him just to see he'd ruined things between them.'' Cole shifted, resting his arm along the top of the couch. ''When Mom found out she was pregnant with me, Cameron just laughed, but Chester offered to marry her. She was scared and alone. Chester was a longtime friend and they'd dated a few times. He'd always loved her from afar, and she was grateful to him." A muscle jumped in Cole's cheek and his smile was bitter. "Chester couldn't have treated me any better if I had been his son. He was good to both of us. But I wish Mom had told me the truth a long time ago."

"Did she say why she kept it a secret for so long?" Annie asked.

He shrugged. "Maybe she thought I'd figure it out. Maria used to tell me I had the same birthmark the Fortunes were all supposed to have, but I never paid much attention to her. I sure didn't ask Mom about it."

Annie remembered remarking on the odd-shaped mark once, but he had shrugged off her interest. "Maybe you realized that questions would be unwelcome," she suggested. "Sometimes children do."

Cole seemed to consider her comment. "Maybe on a subconscious level," he conceded. "The mark was on my back, so I didn't stare at it in a mirror all the time. After a while I forgot it was there."

"Don't expect yourself to accept this all at once," Annie told him. "Finding out you're literally not who you thought you were takes some time to deal with."

"How come you're so smart?" he asked with a wry grin.

She shrugged. "It's just common sense." She wished getting him to accept her going to the Circle A without him would be as easy. After that kiss, sharing a room could be a big mistake, but how could she say no after what he'd just told her?

"We leave the day after tomorrow for the guest ranch," she decided abruptly. "But first we need some rules."

Cole glanced at his watch and got to his feet. "It's late. I still have to unload the truck, and I've got some things to take care of tomorrow if I'm going to be gone from the office. We can work out the logistics on our way to the ranch." Now that he had what he wanted, he was all business. "What time is check-in?"

"Any time after one," Annie replied. Everything was moving too fast, and now she was sorry that she'd given in so easily.

"Great." He headed for the door. "I might as well pick you up. Here or your office?" he asked.

Annie trailed after him, tempted to ask if he was actually going to let her decide something. "I was going to take my car," she said.

Cole chuckled. "That little toy? Where would I sit?"

She wanted to tell him he could sit anywhere he wanted as long as it was here in San Antonio. "That wasn't a problem until you invited yourself," she pointed out instead. "Well, we might as well use your gas. We'll meet at my office."

Cole suggested a time and she agreed. "Got someone to feed your cat?" he asked, surprising her with his sudden concern.

"The neighbor will come over." She tucked her hands into her hip pockets. "There are a few things I want you to understand about this arrangement," she said insistently.

His gaze sharpened. "Don't worry. I know the difference between what's real and what's make-believe."

While Annie was trying to figure out a response to that, he opened the door and went down the steps. Moments later he was gone, leaving a trail of un-answered questions behind as the taillights of his pickup disappeared in the distance. If only the taste of him on her mouth would fade as quickly.

"I thought you told me we were renting a cabin," Cole grumbled to Annie as soon as their hostess, Mrs. Appleberry, finished pointing out the ameni-ties, handed him a printed meal schedule and an activities brochure, then left with a last bright-eyed smile. Unless one counted the bathroom, this was just one good-size room with one very big bed. He'd pictured something more elaborate, with a separate sitting room and an extra couch or even a hide-a-bed.

"I said it was the honeymoon suite," Annie replied, her voice laced with annoyance. "Maybe they figure newlyweds don't need a lot of space." Perhaps she was just as uncomfortable with the setup as he was.

Cole shot her a look, but he didn't dare say anything more. On the silent ride up to the guest ranch, he'd suspected she was having second thoughts about bringing him along, so he'd kept his mouth shut while she made notes on a pad and stared out the window. She'd been chewing on a strand of her hair, something she used to do when she was provoked. For a couple of reasons, he wasn't about to give her an excuse to cancel their little expedition.

"We're both adults," he said now as he tossed his bag on the bed. "I'm sure we can manage."

Annie noticed with a feeling of impending disaster that there didn't appear to be anywhere else in the room comfortable enough to sleep. The interior walls were made from peeled logs, as were the small table and chairs by the window. A wooden love seat with a skimpy calico cushion was placed by a sheepskin in front of the stone fireplace, but she couldn't imagine trying to sleep on it. There was a modern-looking whirlpool bath in the surprisingly luxurious bathroom, or the braided rug by the door. Neither held the appeal of the king-size mattress covered by a fluffy wedding-ring quilt, a ruffled skirt and a heap of pillows.

Since she doubted Cole would be any more willing to stretch out on the floor than she was, it looked as though sharing the bed was their only option. Memories flooded back, memories of falling asleep in his arms, head pillowed on his wide chest and one leg thrown possessively over his.

What if she dropped her guard while she was asleep and woke up plastered against him like a self-stick note? Perhaps she could just stay awake. A couple of days should be more than enough time to find out what she needed to about Clint Lockhart.

Annie opened the tote bag Mrs. Appleberry had insisted on carrying for her, and began putting her clothes in a dresser drawer. "We take all our meals in the dining room," she reminded Cole. "In public, we'll have to act the part of a married couple."

"I think she was suspicious," he replied as he headed into the bathroom with his shaving kit. "She kept looking at us kind of funny."

Annie followed him, still holding the sensible cotton pajamas she'd brought with her. "Who was suspicious?" she demanded.

He set out his gear. "That Mrs. Appleberry. She was watching us like a hawk. She reminds me of an old teacher from junior high, Miss Pitt—she must have been a hundred years old and always looked at the boys like she didn't believe a word we said. I don't think that ring you're wearing is going to fool this gal for long. We'll have to be careful how we act or she could throw us out before you complete your investigation. You said they're very strict here about who they rent to."

"I said they have traditional values." Annie glanced at the birthstone ring she'd put on her left hand. "Women don't wear just diamonds anymore," she added defensively. The sapphire solitaire had been her mother's. "Besides, I didn't think she acted suspicious at all. She was too busy describing all the activities they provide."

"We'll have to be careful if we don't want to draw attention," Cole insisted as he arranged his toiletries in a precise row beside one of the sinks.

Annie narrowed her eyes. "What do you suggest we do?" she asked.

He shrugged as he refolded one of the hand towels and hung it back up on the antique brass bar. "We'll just have to act like we're, uh, that we care about each other."

"Uh-huh," Annie replied, propping one shoulder against the doorjamb and folding her arms. "And how do you propose we do that?"

Cole glanced at her in the mirror over the sink. "I guess we'll just have to follow our instincts." He shifted a basket of individually wrapped guest soaps so it sat exactly halfway between the two sinks.

Annie was tempted to tell him her "instincts" were screaming for her to get the heck out of Dodge and go home, but she had a suspect to investigate. "Whatever you think is necessary," she said sweetly. "Just as long as we don't do anything to tip off Lockhart."

Instantly Cole's expression darkened. "He's trouble."

Yeah, Annie thought, nearly as much trouble as sharing a room with the man she'd once loved, the man who'd kissed her senseless two days ago and who, if she wasn't darn careful, could snap her heart in two like a dry twig, just as he had once before.

"Oh, I'll be careful," she vowed, ignoring his forbidding expression. "But for now, can you clear out of the bathroom? I'd like to freshen up before we case the layout and see if we can find his room."

"Why do you need to know that?" Cole demanded as he brushed past her.

"Like I told you, I'm going to search it for clues while you distract him," Annie said right before she shut the door in his face.

"Annie!" Cole heard the lock *click,* but she didn't reply. He hadn't figured she was really serious about conducting an illegal search. For a moment he stared at the closed door indecisively. Then he heard the water running, so he gave up and went to the window.

He doubted Lockhart would recognize him; they'd never met, and Cole had been gone for six years. Annie had a picture of Lockhart and, just in case he did know who Cole was, they'd checked in under his real name so they wouldn't get caught in a lie.

It seemed strange to share a room with Annie after all this time. They'd gone away together on brief trips once or twice in the past, but they'd both been working too hard to take a real vacation.

Cole tucked his hands into the hip pockets of his old jeans and rocked back on his heels. He'd been stunned when the scandal broke over Annie's head and that of her partner, altering all three of their lives. As soon as Cole had heard, he'd gone to her with every intention of standing by her. It was when he'd asked for a simple explanation that his worst nightmare had begun, and everything between them fell apart.

Now the sound of the bathroom door opening jerked him back to reality. Guiltily, as if she would somehow know what he'd been thinking, he glanced around.

Cole's jaw dropped and he stared, all thoughts of the past driven from his head. Annie had taken down her hair so it spilled over her shoulders and she'd done something to emphasize her eyes. She had changed into a pink knit top that bared a strip of skin above white shorts that looked at least one size too small. Swallowing dryly, he realized he must have deliberately blotted from his mind just how long and sexy those legs of hers really were.

"You look terrific," he finally managed to croak.

Annie parked her hands on her hips, fluttered her lashes and spun around in a circle. "Do you really think so? I want to be sure to catch Lockhart's eye."

Cole's ego deflated like a punctured balloon. "That ought to do it," he grumbled. Unless Texans had changed a lot in the last six years, she'd have every male in the place except the steers and the geldings following her around with their tongues out.

"Terrific!" Annie's pleased smile of response only managed to irritate him further. Apparently oblivious to his annoyance, she unfolded the brochure and studied the map.

"Come on," he growled when he could take no more of their enforced intimacy. "I'm tired of being cooped up in this room." As soon as they got outside, he curved his arm around her shoulders and pulled her close. Annie stiffened as if she'd been turned to stone.

"What are you doing?" she whispered as a couple walking by nodded in their direction.

Cole tipped his head. "I'm acting like your besotted husband," he murmured directly into her ear. The scent of her perfume filled his head, and it was all he could do to keep from burying his face in her hair. For a moment, he nearly forgot where they were.

Annie wriggled against him, turning her head so quickly that their mouths almost collided. "Don't overdo it." Her wide smile didn't reach her eyes. "Even though we're in the honeymoon suite, we don't have to be newlyweds."

Cole was starting to enjoy his role. "Sweetheart, with you, the honeymoon would never end."

Annie stumbled and only his arm kept her from

going down. The moment he realized what he'd said, he let her go. They stared at each other as heat climbed his cheeks and he wished a hawk would fly by and rip out his tongue.

His words roared in Annie's ears like thunder and she couldn't help but wonder if he remembered the last time he'd said that to her—right before they'd broken up. She was about to duck around him and run back into their cabin when she sensed his sudden tension.

"Isn't that him?" he hissed.

Annie barely had time to register that a man wearing a big black Stetson was watching them with interest when Cole wrapped her in his arms, bent her backward and lowered his mouth to hers.

Six

The kiss was short and sweet, and when Cole lifted his head there was a definite gleam in his eyes. Annie had to stop herself from licking his taste from her lips. Instead, she twisted around to catch a glimpse of Clint Lockhart.

"Careful," Cole whispered, pressing her head against his chest. "We don't want to tip him off."

Annie ignored his warning as she struggled to free herself. First he'd taken her by surprise and kissed her; now he was trying to tell her how to do her job. "Where is he?" She searched the gravel path that ran between their cabin and a larger log building. The only likely candidate was the man in the black Stetson, but he didn't look much like the photo.

"It's the guy standing by that tree," Cole replied, his breath caressing her cheek.

"That's not him!" she hissed, disappointed. This man was heavier and his hair, worn long, was the wrong color. "You saw the picture," she told Cole. "How could you think that was Lockhart?"

Cole shrugged. "Sorry. I guess I just panicked." He didn't look the least bit remorseful as he grabbed her hand. "Let's go look around before the dining room opens, *wife*. I'm getting hungry."

Annie searched his face. She'd never known Cole to panic. A dark suspicion was forming. Had he been looking for an excuse to kiss her again? The notion was a heady one, making her dizzy with conflicting emotions. How would she feel if he was interested in her?

Was she *crazy?*

"Annie?" Cole was staring down at her with an expression of concern on his handsome face. His hand tightened on hers. "Are you okay? You went pale. You aren't going to faint, are you?"

She took a deep, steadying breath. What was she thinking? Cole had gotten over his attraction to her years ago. He must really have thought he saw their man.

"I'm fine," she lied, pulling her hand free of his grip. They were supposed to pretend to be married; she couldn't blame Cole for being a good actor. But it *was* only an act. She needed to remember that. "Do you want to look at the snapshot again before we go?" she asked. "I left it in the room."

Was he blushing? No, it had to be the heat, which was plenty warm for October. "I don't think I'll make the same mistake again," he said, cupping his hand under her elbow.

Doing her best to ignore his touch, Annie walked with him toward an open area surrounding two flagpoles. The Stars and Stripes flew from one, and the

tricolored Texas state flag from the other. From
there, more paths fanned out in all directions like
the spokes of a wheel.

Hesitating, she looked around. "Let's go this
way." She pointed toward a long, low building she
assumed was the stable. There was another structure
behind it. "That's not marked on the map in the
brochure. Perhaps it's the employees' bunkhouse."

Cole grabbed her arm. "We can't just go in there
and snoop around. We don't even know which room
is his."

"Of course not. I just want to check out the lo-
cation." Another couple approached them on the
walkway, hand in hand. Immediately Annie sidled
closer to Cole and gazed up at him adoringly. "I
want to see the horses," she cooed in a louder voice.
"There's a trail ride tomorrow." As soon as the
other couple passed them, she dropped her arm.
"Come on." Without waiting to see if he was following, she headed toward the stable, all the while
looking around for Lockhart.

Cole trailed along behind her, enjoying the sun-
shine and the view of her long legs in the white
shorts. When she turned and caught him staring, he
increased his pace and once again grabbed her hand.
This might be his only chance to indulge himself,
and he was going to enjoy every minute of it—all
the while doing his best to keep Annie from taking
any foolish chances.

She was right: the first building was the stable.

The stalls appeared empty, but several horses dozed in an adjacent corral.

"Can I help you?" a man in Western dress asked, touching his fingers to the brim of his hat.

Annie gave him a big smile. "Is that the dorm for single gals?" She pointed at the second building.

"No, ma'am," he replied, following her gaze. "That's where the ranch employees stay. The gals' dorm is over yonder."

"Do you think we could see some real cowboys if we hung around here?" Annie asked.

Ignoring Cole, the man puffed out his chest and hooked his thumbs into his belt loops. "I'm a real cowboy, ma'am."

"Well, of course you are," Annie nearly purred. "Do you bunk there too?"

The man nodded. "All the ranch hands do, except a couple of married guys who've been with the Appleberrys for a long time." He glanced around. "I'm not really supposed to, but I could show you the bunkhouse, if you'd like."

Annie clapped her hands. "Oh, I'd love that." She glanced at Cole, who found her flirtatious technique fascinating to watch. "Honey, why don't you see about a couple of gentle horses for tomorrow's trail ride, and I'll meet you right back here later." Without waiting for a reply, she turned her attention back to the other man. Cole realized he'd been dismissed.

"I'm Annie." She stuck out her hand. "Let's you and me just go on that tour right now."

Looking slightly shell-shocked, the wrangler wrapped his paw around her fingers and introduced himself as Ralph. Annie tucked her hand into the crook of his arm and sashayed away with him, chattering gaily.

Cole watched them for a moment and then stalked toward the stable, torn between irritation and admiration at her cleverness. When her laughter floated back to him, irritation won hands-down.

Annie didn't dare look back to see how Cole was taking her defection. This opportunity had landed in her lap and she had no choice but to take it. Not only would she be able to case the bunkhouse, but she might even get Ralph to show her where Lockhart's room was.

"So where are you from?" Ralph asked as he held open the Dutch door and waited for her to precede him.

The truth was always easier to keep straight than a lie. "Can you believe I live in San Antonio and I've never been to a dude ranch?" Annie asked, batting her lashes. "But I know we're going to have a heavenly time here at the Circle A." Although the hallway, lined with doors and paneled in knotty pine, was rather plain, she looked around with an appreciative smile. "Do you each have your own room or do you share?"

* * *

Cole was still wandering around the stable, keeping an eye out for Lockhart, when he spotted Annie hurrying toward him. From her expression and the high color in her cheeks, he guessed she was in a temper. Apparently she hadn't gotten the information she wanted from Ralph.

Cole walked outside to meet her. "No luck?" he asked when she joined him on the path.

"If you mean, did Ralph get lucky, no he didn't!" she burst out.

"Pardon me?" Cole was confused by the vehemence of her reply. "Did he get out of line?"

Annie took a deep breath. "Forget it. Let's get something to eat," she said, grabbing his arm. "I'm famished."

"What did you mean about Ralph?" Cole persisted as she hustled him toward the dining hall. Other people were headed in the same direction, so he kept his voice low.

"Just because I asked a few questions about employee quarters, that *octopus* assumed I wanted a personal tour of his room," she huffed.

Cole stopped so fast that she nearly tripped. "What happened? Did he hurt you?" If Ralph had so much as touched her—

"I'm fine, but not for lack of trying on his part." Annie's eyes were shooting sparks. "I wanted to see the layout of the bunkhouse, so he showed me his room. And then he didn't want me to leave—and me a married woman, at least as far as he knows.

Can you imagine?'' Apparently she was totally caught up in the role she was playing. Well, Cole wasn't about to force her out of character. Instead, he cuddled her close to his side and dropped a kiss on her hair. Mmm, it smelled like strawberries.

He had to blink away the distraction. ''I think I'd better have a little talk with Ralph,'' he said, glancing behind them. ''I don't think Mrs. Appleberry would approve of his actions toward a paying guest.''

Annie caught at his sleeve. ''No, that's not necessary. We don't want to draw unnecessary attention. I guess I brought it on myself, but I think he's got the right idea now. Besides, I got him to name off several of the other men's quarters, including Lockhart's.''

It took a moment for Cole to absorb what she'd said. When he did, his feelings were mixed. He was committed to proving his mother's innocence, but at what cost? Not Annie's safety.

''I still don't think searching his room is a good idea,'' he argued, even though that was essentially why they'd come. He hadn't given up the hope of changing her mind. ''There must be some other way.''

They reached the line waiting to go into the dining hall and stopped behind another couple who were staring into each other's eyes. Honeymooners, Cole thought.

''Oh, yeah? Like what? Maybe I should just ask

him if he murdered her," Annie suggested outra-
geously.

The honeymooners turned to stare.

"We'll talk about it later, dear," Cole muttered
as a family of four came up behind them.

Dining was family-style with everyone seated at
two long tables. He steered Annie to a couple of
places across from each other and next to the honeymooners, guessing they wouldn't be interested in
small talk. As the meals were served by four attractive young women in old-fashioned gingham checkered dresses, Annie struck up a conversation with
the older couple on their other side.

After introductions all around, the woman, Carol
Best, asked whether Annie and Cole were newly
married.

"Not exactly," Annie replied.

"Yes, we are," Cole said at the same time.

Understandably, Carol looked confused.

Cole slid his arm around Annie's shoulders and
pulled her close. "Actually, we hit a rough patch,"
he confided, "but now we're back on track, aren't
we, honey?"

Annie stiffened in his embrace. Her smile was
brittle and her eyes shot daggers. "We sure are,
sugar." Her voice dripped sarcasm that he hoped no
one else noticed.

One of the waitresses served plates of chicken-
fried steak, baked beans and coleslaw as the other
brought out baskets of rolls and took their beverage

order. Conversation died when Mrs. Appleberry appeared at the end of one table to give a brief blessing. As soon as she was done, everyone began to eat.

"Are you two going to the dance class later?" Carol asked after a moment.

"We'll probably check it out," Annie replied before Cole could say anything. "The brochure promised that some of the cowboys will be on hand to demonstrate the steps." No doubt she hoped to spot Lockhart among them.

"Speaking of demonstrations," Carol's husband said, leaning closer, "there's a trick roping and riding demonstration in the outdoor arena later, right before the campfire and sing-along. All the ranch hands participate."

Cole and Annie exchanged glances. "Sounds like an opportunity we wouldn't want to miss," she said.

Cole's stomach lurched. He knew what she had in mind. "I thought we were going to take a walk in the moonlight tonight," he protested, hoping she wouldn't want to argue in front of the other couple.

Annie patted his cheek. "There will be plenty of time for that too," she told him in a voice loaded with promise.

As soon as they finished the apple pie and ice cream that was served the moment the lunch plates were cleared, Annie made arrangements to meet the Bests at the dance lesson. She looked elated as she and Cole left the dining room.

"I'm going to gain ten pounds while we're here," she complained, patting her flat stomach.

"Why did you agree to meet them?" Cole asked. "I thought it would be fun to take out a couple of the horses. You used to enjoy riding, and we might as well have a little fun while we're here." He was beginning to think trying to learn anything about Clint was futile.

"We aren't here to have fun," Annie reminded him as she led the way to their room. "Lockhart may be one of the men partnering the female guests. From what I've heard, that kind of thing would be right up his alley."

"Why do we care if he knows the steps to the latest line dance?" Cole grumbled.

"We don't. I want to get a good look at him so I'll be sure to recognize him right away if I see him later."

"You mean if you run into him coming out of his room?" Cole asked.

"Exactly." Annie waited by their front door while he unlocked it. If she thought she was getting her way without another argument from him she was mistaken.

"How do you plan on pulling this off?" he asked after he'd shut the door behind them. It was cooler inside. Overhead a ceiling fan circled lazily. "Don't you think anyone will notice a female guest sneaking around the employee quarters trying to break into one of the rooms?"

Without bothering to reply, Annie took a small bag from the dresser drawer, laid it on the bed and unzipped it. She extracted what Cole assumed were lock-picking tools as well as a pager, a small cell phone and a tiny camera that looked like a toy. "Everyone will be at the riding and roping demonstration this evening," she said. "I checked with Mrs. Appleberry. It's a big draw and all the male employees are expected to participate. You'll be there, keeping an eye on Lockhart. If he leaves before I come out, you can page me."

Cole contemplated her plan, searching for flaws. "What if someone sees you and wonders what you're doing?" he asked.

"I'll say I was looking for Ralph."

"The guy who came on to you earlier?" Cole exclaimed.

"Relax. I don't plan on getting caught," Annie told him as she held up the picks. "All I need is about a minute and I'm in." She gave him a level look. "Can I count on you to help me with this or not?"

Cole raked his fingers through his hair. It was obvious that her mind was made up. All he could do was make damn sure she didn't get caught. "Okay," he growled. "Give me the damn cell phone."

A half-hour later, after Annie had freshened her makeup, spritzed on more perfume and changed to a cropped top with fringe around the bottom, she put the equipment she'd shown him in a fanny pack and tucked it back into the drawer. They both studied Lockhart's photo again and then they left their room, locking the door carefully behind them and following the sound of music to the covered area where the dance lessons were being held. Cole insisted on holding her hand on the way, but the contact didn't bother her. Instead she decided to enjoy it. They were pretending to be a couple; what harm could a little fantasizing on her part do? Besides, even though she wouldn't have admitted it even if she'd been staked to an ant hill, she was glad he was here with her.

This time when Cole whispered that he saw Lockhart, she spotted him too. He was leaning against the wall with several other men, all decked out in genuine cowboy garb, including boots and Stetsons. Along with the toothpick stuck in the corner of his mouth, Lockhart wore a confident smile as he scanned the group of guests. He was attractive in a rough sort of way, but a shiver of warning trickled down Annie's spine. When his gaze caught her eye, she curved her lips into a smile before she looked quickly away.

Cole had no idea about the first part of her plan. When the Bests waved from a table for four on the edge of the open dance floor, Annie let him lead her over and hold out her chair. Carol greeted them cheerfully, but Roger Best looked as though he would rather be somewhere else.

"We're missing the branding demonstration in the corral," he told Cole glumly.

Carol poked her husband playfully. "This will be more fun. You'll see."

Roger didn't look as though he believed her.

Cole's back was to Lockhart, but Annie was facing him. Once again she caught his eye over Cole's shoulder and gave him a long look, but she didn't risk a smile this time. After all, she was supposed to be with her husband.

Pretty soon an older man came out and introduced himself to the group as Glen Appleberry. Below his Adam's apple was a bolo tie with a chunk of turquoise the size of a hen's egg. His belt buckle looked like a headlight and his boots were snake-skin.

Glen and his wife demonstrated the basic steps of the first dance they'd be doing, the Western Swing. Then they invited everyone to join them on the floor.

"Don't be shy," he urged when no one moved. "There are plenty of experienced partners here to help, if you're new at this. A couple of turns around the floor with one of our Circle A experts, and you'll be ready to dance with your spouse or sweetheart like a pro."

The personnel leaning against the wall, including Clint Lockhart and the waitresses from lunch, began approaching the guests, hands extended. Just as Annie had hoped, Lockhart made a beeline for her.

He stopped in front of Cole and tipped his hat. "Okay with you if I dance with the lady?" he asked deferentially.

Cole glowered. For a moment she was afraid he was going to refuse. "It's up to her," he said finally.

Annie saw a triumphant gleam in Lockhart's eye that was quickly smothered as he took her hand. He was wearing leather gloves. Introducing himself and asking her name, he led her to the far side of the floor.

"Call me Annie," she replied with a wide smile as the music started up again. Out of the corner of her eye, she saw a pretty blonde tug playfully on Cole's hand until he got to his feet. A twinge of jealousy distracted Annie, and she missed what Clint was saying.

Before she realized what was happening, he'd put an arm around her and was walking her through the steps of the dance. With a big effort, Annie tore her attention away from Cole so she could set out to soften up her partner.

"Is that your husband?" he asked.

She nodded, concentrating on her feet.

"Been married long?" he persisted, holding her too tightly.

"Too long," she agreed with a light laugh. "What about you?"

His grin was confident. "Nah, I've avoided that noose. Never wanted to be tied down."

Annie wondered if that was what had gone wrong with Sophia. Had she pressured him to make a commitment? "You must have lots of women after you," she said with an appreciative glance after he swung her around. "A handsome cowboy like you wouldn't have to be alone if he didn't want to be."

He shrugged. "You could say my last relationship ended rather abruptly," he drawled with a grin that chilled Annie to the bone. "The woman's not around anymore."

Was he joking about Sophia? It was all Annie could do to keep her repulsion from showing. She could be dancing with a cold-blooded killer.

"What was your girlfriend's name?" she asked daringly.

In a blink his eyes went flat and cold. "It's not important."

Annie didn't dare dig any deeper for fear of making him suspicious. Instead she pretended to stumble. "Sorry," she exclaimed, falling heavily against him.

Lockhart held her close for a moment too long before he let her go. "No problem," he said smoothly as he stared into her eyes. "You're sure a pretty thing."

Cole had managed to maneuver the waitress near them. It was all he could do to keep himself from abandoning the little blonde and charging to Annie's

rescue the moment he saw Lockhart give her a hug
that wasn't part of the dance. If the man hadn't almost immediately released her again, Cole probably
would have made a fool of himself and ruined her
plan as well.

"Are you okay?" the waitress asked as he
whipped her forcefully around like a yo-yo on a
string.

"Sorry." He clutched at the distraction. "Maybe
you'd better demonstrate this step again." Although
he tried hard to concentrate, he was relieved when
the music ended and there was an exodus from the
floor. By the time he'd thanked her and worked his
way back to the table, Lockhart was already there
with Annie.

"I'll take it from here," Cole said, pulling out
her chair.

Her mouth tightened with annoyance and then she
flashed Lockhart a smile that set Cole's jaw muscles.
Before she sat down, she leaned toward the other
man and murmured something Cole couldn't hear.

Lockhart winked and then he glanced at Cole.
"Have fun," he said to both of them with a smirk,
and then he backed away. Annie finally sat down as
the music was starting again, but Cole sure didn't
feel like dancing. The couple sharing their table
hadn't come back after the last number. They were
still on the floor holding hands. Apparently Roger
had changed his mind about the branding.

"Let's get out of here," Cole said to Annie.

"You got what you came for." From her expression and the stiff set he could feel on his own face he figured anyone who noticed would assume they were quarreling. It would be natural for them to leave.

For a moment he thought she'd refuse, but then she surprised him by getting to her feet. "You're right," she replied with a toss of her head. "There's no point in staying."

As Annie threaded her way among the small tables, she saw Lockhart watching her. No doubt his arrogance would lead him to assume they were arguing about him. The man was repellent and all she wanted was a shower, but she wasn't about to admit that to Cole. She knew he was acting, but his interpretation of a jealous spouse was Oscar material. If she wasn't careful, she'd forget it was all a pretense.

"That went well," she said as they entered their quarters.

Cole's sound of disbelief made her stare. "I didn't know my role was going to be the cuckolded husband. Keep playing with Lockhart and you won't need your lock picks to get into his room." He sounded furious.

"What are you suggesting?" Annie demanded, put on the defensive.

Cole glared. "I think a smart girl like you can figure that out."

He was carrying his role too far. "I'm going to take a shower," she announced haughtily as she grabbed clean clothes and swept past him. "If you want to know the truth, after dealing with the two of you, I feel like I need one."

Cole looked stunned. Without giving him a chance to reply, she went into the bathroom and locked the door behind her. Men!

When she came back out a little while later, wearing a broomstick skirt in a pastel flowered print and a seafoam-green sleeveless blouse, he was stretched out on the bed with his hands behind his head.

"I'm sorry," he said without preamble. "I don't know what got into me."

"I guess you just immersed yourself in your part," Annie replied. It seemed like all they did was quarrel and apologize. Cautiously she sat on the edge of the bed with the intention of going over the evening's plans with him.

"You look nice," he said. "You're still one of the prettiest women I've ever seen."

It was all she could do to keep her mouth from dropping open. What was he up to? He'd never been big on compliments in the old days. "Thank you," she stammered.

Tension crackled between them. If the truth be told, with his black hair and blue eyes, Cole was by far the most physically attractive man she'd known. Perhaps the reason she'd never again gotten seriously involved was because no other man appealed to her as strongly as he had. Cole had been her first and only lover. Sharing a room reminded her of the times they'd been together—

Annie quickly got up from the bed and sat down a safer distance away from temptation. It was either that or stretch out next to him. Wouldn't that be a shock? Perhaps she could tell him it was method acting, that she was submersing herself in her role.

"Why did you move?" he asked, propping himself up on one elbow. "I didn't mean to make you uncomfortable. Surely other men have complimented you on your looks."

If it was meant as a question, it wasn't one she was going to answer. Let him wonder.

When she didn't respond, he sat up and smoothed his hair with one hand. "Are we ever going to talk about what happened?"

"With Lockhart?" she asked. "I told you I'm going to search his room during the riding and roping exhibition."

"Don't play dumb," Cole said impatiently. "You know what I meant. There's still something between us. I could feel it when you kissed me. Are we ever going to discuss the past?"

Annie leaped to her feet and crossed to the window, huddling there with her arms folded protectively across her chest. "The past is over and done with," she said, gazing through the curtain without really seeing anything. "It's the present we should both be focused on—finding Sophia's real murderer and clearing your mother." She turned and looked at him, willing him to stay where he was while she dealt with the panic his suggestion raised inside her. Instead, he got to his feet and came toward her, watching her closely with an unreadable expression.

"Ryan says you're the best investigator around," he said softly, stopping right in front of her. "Smart, brave, clever. Willing to do whatever is necessary for a successful investigation. Do you really know what you're doing now?"

Annie wanted to take that one last step that would close the gap between them. *No,* she wanted to shout. *I don't have any idea what I'm doing. All I want is to stay in this room with you and forget all about the outside world.*

She needed to have her head examined. The past she tried so hard to ignore rose between them like an ugly specter, reminding her to be careful.

"I know exactly what I'm doing," she said in a cool voice, "and it's all strictly business." Stepping around him, she retrieved her fanny pack from the dresser and sat back down in the wooden chair. Methodically she double-checked its contents. "Right now we need to review our plan for this evening so neither of us makes a misstep that could tip off our quarry or get someone hurt."

After a moment Cole joined her at the table. His jaw was clenched and a muscle flexed in his cheek. His gaze was steady on hers. "Show me what you want me to do."

Seven

As Annie made her way to the employee bunk-house early that evening, she was relieved to see that her hunch had been right. Everyone appeared to have gone to the exhibition down at the outdoor arena. She could hear bursts of cheering and applause. Cole was there and he'd already paged her once to let her know he had Lockhart in his sights.

Adrenaline bubbled through her veins as she deliberately slowed her pace on the off-chance someone might see her and question her intentions. The last thing she wanted was to appear furtive. She'd learned long ago how important it was to blend in, to act as though everything was ordinary and routine.

Annie quenched a smile. For her this *was* routine.

In moments she was inside the building, headed for the room Ralph had so helpfully pointed out.

She listened, but all was quiet except for the now-fainter noise from outside. Taking a deep breath, she drew her picks from her pack and went to work. She hadn't lost her touch and the lock was no challenge; in less than a minute she was inside.

Heart pounding, she leaned against the closed door and looked around the empty room. The heavy curtains were drawn against the fading light, so it took a moment for her eyes to adjust. She had a flashlight tucked into her pocket, but she hated taking the risk of being noticed if she didn't have to.

As well as being a slimeball and a murder suspect, Lockhart was also a slob. The narrow bed was a tangle of sheets and blankets. Clothes were scattered all over the floor and heaped on a chair. With a shudder of distaste, Annie stepped over a pair of underwear. The dresser was covered with an assortment of loose change, playing cards, beer bottles, unopened mail and other clutter.

Methodically she began searching for anything that might link him to Sophia's death. Even though the fruits of Annie's search couldn't be used in court, she might find something, anything, that would give her a clue. Although the prosecutor had to share his information with the defense, the deal wasn't reciprocal. It was one of the little quirks of criminal law that Annie didn't mind at all.

Swiftly she made a visual search and then went through the dresser drawers, careful to put everything back the way she found it. She found a jumble of underwear, socks, a couple of bandanna handkerchiefs, a belt and an extra pair of leather gloves. In the back of the drawer was a small manila envelope. She looked inside.

Newspaper clippings! With a speeding pulse, Annie pulled them out and glanced through them. Several were starting to yellow. Puzzled, she skimmed each one carefully, mindful of the passage of time. They were all about Bryan Fortune's kidnapping, from the time he first disappeared until the most recent ransom note was found. She wouldn't have pegged Lockhart as the kind of man to take such an interest in family business that didn't concern him directly, even when it was such a tragedy. Reluctantly, feeling as though she was missing something right under her nose, Annie put the clippings back in the envelope and returned them to the drawer.

Pushing it shut, she resumed her search. On a small table by the bed were a dusty brass lamp with a stained shade, an overflowing ashtray, a silver buckle inlaid with turquoise and two books of matches. In the closet were several shirts and a couple of fancy Western-cut jackets on hangers, a pale gray Stetson on the shelf and a dressy pair of boots on the floor next to a battered duffel bag.

When Annie had checked everything else, she upended the silver-toed boots. One was empty, but a small package wrapped in a red bandanna fell out of the other. In it were a fancy gold necklace with a broken link and a pawn ticket. Swiftly she laid the necklace on the bed on a clean white handkerchief she'd brought for the purpose and snapped a couple of pictures of it with her camera. The pawn ticket she studied for a moment and then slipped into a clear plastic bag. The necklace she wrapped in the bandanna. Which boot had it been in? She finally dropped it back into the left one. All she could do was hope Lockhart didn't miss the ticket anytime soon.

In the bathroom, messy enough to make her cringe, she removed a few hairs from his brush, just in case, and slipped them into another bag. Although she searched the counter and the cabinet beneath the sink, she found nothing else useful. As she was returning his shaving kit to the drawer, her pager vibrated against her hip.

Lockhart was coming! Knowing she might only have a moment or two, she got down on her hands and knees for a quick peek beneath the bed. Nothing there but dust and a wool boot sock with a hole in the toe. When she got back up, she glanced at the open closet door. Had it been shut when she arrived? No time to decide.

With a last visual sweep of the bedroom to make sure she'd left nothing behind, she eased open the door and peeked out. The corridor was empty. Her pager vibrated again, making her jump. Was Cole trying to tell her something, or just being excessively cautious?

Taking a deep breath, she slid out of the room, pulled the door shut behind her and hurried down the hall. Unfortunately there was only one way out. As she turned a corner, she nearly slammed into Lockhart.

"Hey!" Obviously surprised, he grabbed her

arms as she skidded to a stop. "What are you doing here?" His gaze narrowed suspiciously. "Why aren't you at the show? I spotted your husband there."

"Why aren't *you?*" Annie countered, with what she hoped was a sexy grin. Her heart was pounding so hard she wondered if he could hear it. They were alone. What if he got curious about the pack around her waist and wanted to see inside?

She'd ordered Cole to stay the heck away from the bunkhouse, but now she wished he would appear. It wasn't that she needed rescuing, but backup would have been nice.

Lockhart released her to hold up one hand. His leather glove was split along the side seam. "Just came back to get my other pair," he replied. Then he stretched out his arm and planted his hand on the wall by her head, effectively blocking her escape. His gaze sharpened.

"You didn't tell me what you were doing here," he pointed out.

His breath was stale, making Annie want to bolt. How had she thought he was attractive, even in a rough way? "I was looking for you," she forced herself to purr as she ran one finger down the front of his leather vest.

How could he fall for anything so blatant? He knew she was married and that her husband might very well be wondering where she was.

"Oh, yeah?" For a moment he stared at her with

a mix of suspicion and male arrogance stamped on his features. To both her relief and dismay, arrogance must have won. He smiled and leaned closer. Like the flick of a snake's tongue, his gaze darted to her mouth and then back to her eyes. His grin turned gloating.

"Getting a little bored with the home fires, are you?" he drawled.

Annie's stomach lurched. She fluttered her lashes. "Does it show?" she pouted, easing back until her head hit the wall behind her. Just how far would she have to carry this little charade before someone else came along to interrupt them or Lockhart decided a rendezvous in the hallway might be too risky? From his expression, caution probably wasn't high on his list of character traits.

"I haven't bored any women yet," he bragged.

She thought of Sophia, and her knees wobbled. Had killing her been an impulsive act, triggered by a temper that didn't deal well with rejection?

Again Annie wished she'd gone with her instincts instead of trying to show Cole her all-fired independence. "I'll just bet you haven't," she responded lamely. Maybe she could stall Lockhart, suggest they meet later. To her horror, he glanced around and then pulled out his room key.

"Come on," he said, hooking an arm around Annie's waist and jerking her closer. "No one will notice that I'm gone for a few extra minutes."

For a moment, her mind went blank as he started

hustling her back down the way she'd just come. A woman, even one trained in self-defense as she had been, could still be at a disadvantage with a bigger and stronger male.

Merciful heavens, but his arrogance was unbelievable. Did he actually think she'd go with him for some kind of crude five-minute quickie?

Obviously he did. He was doing his damnedest to get her inside his room, and he was surprisingly strong. She'd underestimated him. Before she could formulate an excuse and bolt, he had her sandwiched between him and his door while he fumbled with the lock.

It was now or never. She wasn't about to be raped just to preserve her cover! In a near panic, she shoved his hand away from the knob. Instantly his head snapped up, his triumphant smile replaced by an even uglier expression.

"What's your game, lady?" he growled. This time when he grabbed her arm, his grip hurt.

Gritting her teeth, Annie shifted away. Her breasts brushed his chest and it was all she could do to keep from gagging. Instead she licked her lips and forced a smile of her own. As much as she'd like the satisfaction of taking him down, talking her way out of this would be the best way to handle it.

"Your seduction technique could use a little work," she teased. "I'm not some carcass to be dragged off to your lair."

To her relief, his hold on her arm eased up

slightly. He stepped closer, pinning her against the wall. "You came after me," he reminded her in a hoarse voice as he ground his hips against hers. She realized he was aroused.

Fury whipped through Annie. To hell with sweet talk. No one treated her like this!

Lockhart dipped his head and she was about to resort to physical force when she saw a movement out of the corner of her eye.

Cole!

"What the hell is going on here?" he demanded with righteous indignation worthy of a genuine betrayed husband. At the same time he grabbed Lockhart by the shoulder and spun him away from Annie, who sagged with relief.

"Get your hands off me!" Lockhart reacted with unexpected speed, hitting Cole in the chest. Annie let out a shriek as his fist connected with Lockhart's mouth, snapping his head back. As he staggered and nearly went down, the owner of the Circle A, Glen Appleberry, came hurrying around the corner.

"Good grief, what's this all about?" he demanded, face going instantly red when he saw Cole's expression and Lockhart's bloody lip.

Before either of the younger men could speak, Annie hurled herself into Mr. Appleberry's arms. "Thank goodness you're here!" she exclaimed, bursting into tears of relief that weren't totally staged.

"Mrs. Cassidy," he said, prying her off him,

"what on earth are you doing in the employee dorm?"

Good question, and one she certainly didn't want him to pursue. "This man assaulted me," she wailed, squeezing out more tears. "I was just wandering around and he g-grabbed me. Thank goodness my husband came along or I don't know what might have happened."

To her embarrassment, two more ranch hands showed up, apparently drawn by the noise. Behind them were several guests! Cole was watching her with a thunderous frown that appeared way too real, and Lockhart looked as though he would have liked to kill her.

Oh, dear. This was getting out of hand.

"Don't listen to her," Lockhart exclaimed. "I just came to get my other gloves. This broad ambushed me. She said she was looking for me. Next thing I know, she's all over me like a cat in heat."

Annie's cheeks flamed. Swearing, Cole lunged at him, but she managed to get between the straining male bodies and flash Cole a warning look. The smartest thing now would be a hasty retreat, before Mr. Appleberry could ask too many questions.

"Touch her again and you'll regret it," Cole told Lockhart despite Annie's unspoken warning.

To her shock, the guest ranch owner reached up and grabbed Lockhart by the nape of the neck with a surprising show of strength.

"You've been warned before about bothering the

female guests," he thundered, giving the younger
man a hard shake as he struggled like a fish on a
hook. "Pack your gear and clear out."

"Um..." Annie started, and then she fell silent
again. Oh, hell, all she wanted now was to get away
without arousing suspicion. Judging from the interested expressions on the faces of those in the small
group around them, and the pure hatred in Lockhart's eyes, the chance of that happening was fading
fast.

Mr. Appleberry glanced at her and then at Cole.
"I'm dreadfully sorry this happened," he said. "If
the two of you will come to my office in a little
while, we'll straighten it all out." He glared at
Lockhart. "Just as soon as I write this man a sev-
erance check and have him escorted to the gate,"
he added.

"That's not fair," Lockhart whined. "It's her
word against mine."

"Her word and that of several other women,"
Appleberry retorted, and then he looked as though
he could have bitten his tongue. He looked at one
of the other employees standing off to the side.
"Stan, keep an eye on our friend here, will you?"

"Sure thing, boss." The man called Stan came
forward and grabbed Lockhart's elbow. "You heard
him," he said, holding out his other hand. "Give
me your key and let's get your stuff packed."

With a last venomous glance at Annie and Cole,
Lockhart complied.

"Okay, folks," Appleberry said, rubbing his hands together briskly. "The campfire and sing-along will be starting shortly. Why don't you all head back to the arena. We'll be serving complementary beverages and popcorn in just a little while." As soon as the small crowd had dispersed, he put a hand on Annie's shoulder and one on Cole's, herding them toward the door.

"Are you all right?" Appleberry asked Annie as soon as they were all outside. "He didn't actually hurt you, did he?"

She shook her head. "I'm okay, really. My husband came along just in time." She let a shudder go through her. It wasn't difficult. "All I want is to go to my room and lie down."

"I'd like to talk to you whenever you're up to it," he said, including Cole in his glance. "But perhaps you'd rather wait until morning."

"That would be fine." Cole spoke for the first time since he'd threatened Lockhart. "My wife needs a chance to get over this. We'll see you after breakfast."

All Annie wanted was to get away from the bunkhouse before Lockhart came back out. "Good idea," she agreed. "I think I'll just go take a bath in that lovely whirlpool." It was the first thing she could think of, but a soak did sound heavenly. She needed to get *clean.* Impatiently she tugged on Cole's arm. "Come on, honey. Let's go."

Apparently Cole was no more eager for another

confrontation with Lockhart than she was. They bid their host a hasty good-night and headed back to their room, Annie's hand firmly in Cole's.

She expected him to ask about her search as soon as they were out of earshot. Instead he stopped and turned to her on the path.

"Are you really okay?" he asked, touching her cheek with his fingers. "I'm so damn sorry I didn't get there any sooner."

Annie realized it wasn't the time to tell him she hadn't *really* been in danger unless one counted being nauseated, that if she'd had to she could have immobilized Lockhart with any number of aggressive physical moves. Instead she smiled up at Cole, a wave of tenderness welling inside her. "Thank you for getting there when you did." She was perfectly sincere when she added, "I was never so glad to see anyone in my life."

Eyes dark with emotion, he managed a crooked smile. "Thank God he didn't hurt you. When I first saw you with him, I wanted to tear him apart."

Annie didn't know what to say to that, so she started walking instead, glad the whole experience was behind her. As they reached their room and went inside, she waited for him to ask about the mission. The room was growing darker, but neither of them bothered with a lamp. Instead Cole lit a fat candle sitting on the hearth and one on the nightstand. They cast a warm, comforting glow over the rustic setting, and Annie appreciated the gesture.

Cole was acting as though her safety and comfort were more important to him than anything else. For a moment she allowed herself to bask in the idea that she really mattered to him, and then she sank onto the edge of the bed as her knees went weak.

To her surprise, he came over and sat beside her, turning so he could search her face in the candlelight. What she saw in his eyes made her tremble, and then he put his arms around her. Sighing, she laid her head on his shoulder as he held her gently. For a long time they sat that way, not moving, not talking, while she let the warmth from his body soak into her. Finally, with great reluctance, she straightened and smiled at him.

"I'm okay now," she said.

Cole cleared his throat. "What nearly happened back there made me realize something very important." He was so close she could feel his breath on her cheek.

"What's that?" she asked, mesmerized by his nearness. Already the memory of the unpleasant scene with Lockhart was starting to fade. The tightly coiled knot of tension in her stomach began to relax, replaced by another kind of awareness that hummed pleasantly along her nerves.

"I want to be with you," Cole murmured. "I want this night with you to be real, not make-believe."

There were a dozen questions that needed asking, a hundred memories that should be dealt with, a thousand painful moments Annie had suffered through after Cole left. Not one of them had the power to keep her from taking the gift of this night.

Before she could respond, Cole turned his face away. "I'm sorry," he rasped. "You were very nearly assaulted and now *I'm* hitting on you." He got to his feet without looking at her. "You probably want to be alone for a while—take that bath you mentioned. I'll go for a walk, give you some privacy."

When he glanced at her again, his expression was grim, his eyes dark with hunger and remorse. "Forget what I said, okay? I'll be back after a while."

Without taking the time to consider the eventual consequences, Annie went to him and slid her arms around his neck. It would have been easy to tell herself she was using him to erase the unpleasant memory of Lockhart grinding himself against her, but she didn't.

She wanted Cole. It was that simple.

"I don't need privacy," she told him, tipping back her head and looking into his face. "I need *you.*"

With a muffled groan, he swept her into his arms and covered her mouth with his. Long and hard he kissed her, obliterating reason and replacing it with a burning ache that was impossible to ignore. Caught up in the storm of emotion breaking around them, Annie opened her mouth on a sigh and melted

into him. No one had ever aroused the feelings in
her that Cole did so easily.

Being with him like this was a breathtaking swirl
of both brand-new and familiar sensations. For a
moment she faltered as memories of other kisses,
other times with him, swept through her with the
force of a prairie fire. Clinging fiercely to him, she
refused to allow those memories to take away from
the here and now.

"I've missed you," he groaned, and she chose to
believe him.

"I've missed *you*," she echoed, meaning it with
every fiber of her being. Six long years were compressed more surely into nothingness with each kiss,
each touch. Six long years compressed itself to no
more than a heartbeat and then to a blink. By the
time he lifted her into his arms, she was just as
deeply in love with him as she had ever been.

Gently Cole laid her on the bed. He stared into
her eyes, misty with desire, and his heart did a lazy
barrel roll. Later, he promised himself, they would
talk, sort through everything. For now the words ran
together in his head like the colors in a rainbow. He
meant to be slow and oh, so expert in his wooing,
to savor each moment between them and to erase
the memory of other lovers from her mind. Instead,
when she sighed his name and opened her arms,
emotion crashed through him like a tidal wave.

Wrapping her in his embrace, he rolled so she was
above him on the wide bed. He stared into her face,

savoring each dear feature in the glow from the bed-side candle. In one swift movement she separated the snaps on his shirt and lowered her head. The touch of her mouth on his bare skin pushed him closer to the edge. Fighting for control, he coaxed her shirt over her head and unclasped her bra.

Her breasts spilled into his hands. When he squeezed them gently, caressing her with fingers that trembled, she whispered his name. Her nipples had always been sensitive and she had loved for him to touch them. Urging her closer, he took the sweet bounty into his mouth. Her low moan was wildly exciting. When she shifted against him, drawing her legs up so that she was kneeling, he arched into her welcoming heat.

Vaguely Cole realized they were both still half dressed. His trembling hands tightened on the bare skin above her waist. If he didn't get inside her, he was going to explode.

Annie lifted her head. With a secretive grin she wiggled down his body while he struggled for re-straint.

"Witch," he groaned when she began working on the buckle of his belt. Her soft laughter brought back a slew of memories, spiking his desire. Some-how they managed to deal with the rest of each other's clothes, Cole fumbling with his boots and socks. By then Annie was completely undressed and even lovelier than he remembered. She'd been slim before, but now her body was strong and supple, her curves matured in a way that stole his breath.

He wanted to tell her so, but he was afraid to bring up their shared history in any way. The last thing he wanted was to taint the present with shadows from the past. Besides, if she called a halt now, he would probably die of sheer frustration. He'd never wanted a woman as much as he wanted Annie right this minute.

Annie was watching all the while, and from the look of approval on her face, she still found him attractive as well.

"Come here," Cole invited, stretching out and opening his arms. When she closed the distance between them, crawling across the mattress with cat-like grace, he poured everything he was feeling into a passionate kiss. Annie matched his passion with an openness that was astonishingly sexy.

Moments later, when Cole claimed her, he wondered how his heart could handle the overload of feelings surging through him. Truly he'd come home. Then his brain shut down and he was pulled into a vortex of passion. She cried his name. Together they spun out of control, racing toward the sun and beyond.

Boneless, drifting, Annie let her arms drop from around Cole's shoulders as she waited for her heartbeat to slow. He was collapsed beside her. Making love had always seemed to knock him sideways, sapping his strength. She'd loved that vulnerability in him. Now the only sound in the room was the rasp of their combined breathing.

As that first euphoric high began to ebb, she could feel his gaze, and she wondered what he was thinking. From outside there was a shout, followed by a burst of laughter. The noise brought Annie back to reality.

What in Sam Hill had they done? What had she been *thinking?* Cole had crooked his finger, and she'd fallen into his arms like an overripe peach.

"Annie?" The mattress shifted beneath his weight.

Confused, dismayed, she turned onto her side away from him. Doubts began circling and buzzing in her head like killer bees.

"Are you okay?" His voice was low, puzzled.

Unable to find her own voice, she nodded. Her bareness made her feel even more vulnerable, so she sat up, swinging her legs over the opposite edge of the bed, and looked for her clothes. Unfortunately they were on the floor out of her reach.

"Damn," Cole muttered, pulling himself into a sitting position propped against the headboard. As she slanted him a glance, he raked his fingers through his hair, leaving it spiky. "I'm sorry. I should have realized you were too upset."

He reached out and touched her shoulder with his fingertips, but she flinched away. The last thing she wanted was for him to suspect how very much he'd affected her. And she didn't need his pity.

"I'm fine," she said in a brittle voice. "Don't be sorry. We always were good together, weren't we?" She managed to face him. He was frowning. Maybe it hadn't been good for him. A knife went through her, making her painfully aware just how chilling was the power he still wielded over her.

"Cole?" she asked.

Slowly, as though not to spook her, he leaned forward and captured her wrist. "We have to talk."

How desperately she wanted to curl up against him with her ear pressed to his chest so she could hear the rumble of his voice. Instead she pulled away and got to her feet. Resisting the urge to cover herself, she kept her hands at her sides.

"We're unattached adults," she replied with a shaky laugh. "Circumstances threw us together. No need for a postmortem, is there?"

If he apologized again, she'd either hit him or burst into tears. Didn't men know anything? She was allowed to regret what had happened, but he'd better not admit to one measly doubt or he was worse than pond scum! It was a rule.

"Not a postmortem," he replied, looking worried. "It's just that we can't move ahead until we deal with the past, once and for all."

Panic welled in Annie. No way was she going to rehash that, not when she was emotionally turned inside out from the sheer power of what they had just shared. "We're not moving anywhere," she said bluntly as she bolted for the bathroom. "This was just an interlude, and now I'm taking that bath I promised myself."

Before Cole could stop her, she'd slipped through the doorway, switched on the bathroom light and turned the lock behind her.

Ignoring his protests, she stood blinking against the sudden brightness. Then she turned the faucets on full force, muffling the sound of his voice, and emptied half a jar of bubble bath into the whirlpool. By the time she had to turn the water off or risk filling the entire room with bubbles, all was quiet in the other room.

Annie pressed her ear to the door, but she heard nothing. Had he gone to sleep? Dressed and gone for a walk? It was a warm night.

Refusing to face the thoughts and feelings squirreling through her brain, clamoring for attention, she stepped into the tub. As she did, she realized that she still hadn't told him what she found in Lockhart's room. Even more surprising, Cole hadn't thought to ask.

Eight

Cole had pulled on his jeans and was sitting in a chair by the window when Annie finally opened the bathroom door. Although the sun had been down for a long time now, he still hadn't bothered switching on the lamps. The soft glow from the candles was somehow comforting. Maybe the shadows were just a good place to hide from his feelings about what had happened between them.

Making love to Annie had stirred up emotions he would have sworn he dealt with and put aside years ago.

"Cole?" There was uncertainty in her voice as she stood silhouetted in the bathroom doorway, wrapped in a thick terry robe provided by the guest ranch.

"I'm right here," he said, in case her eyes hadn't adjusted to the change in the light.

She opened the door wider and stepped into the room as cautiously as a deer approaching a watering hole. "I'm done in here. Sorry I took so long."

When he finished his shower and came back out ten minutes later, a towel wrapped around his waist, she was standing by the window. "You didn't ask if I'd found anything in Lockhart's room," she said abruptly as he switched off the bathroom light.

"I guess I had other things on my mind." His voice was edged with irony, but he couldn't help it. Just as he'd feared, one taste of Annie hadn't been enough to douse the fire that burned inside him. Even while she reminded him why they were really here, his body clamored to possess her once more.

She padded across the room, her bare feet nearly soundless, and picked up the pack she'd worn earlier.

Setting it on the table, she switched on a small brass lamp and pulled up a chair.

"So what did you find?" He sat down across from her, curiosity whetted.

Annie worked the zipper as slowly as a stripper peeling off her dress, finally removing the camera and a piece of paper. "I need to get this film developed in the morning," she said. "I took pictures of a necklace he'd hidden in his boot, and I want to see if Ryan or Lily recognize it."

"What's this?" Cole asked, poking at the other item that lay facedown on the table.

"A pawn ticket." Annie turned it over. "The shop's in San Antonio, so I'll check it out tomorrow too. Who knows, it could lead to something."

Cole's shoulders slumped with disappointment. What had he expected—a journal containing Lockhart's written confession? "Did you see anything else while you were there?" he asked.

"Just some newspaper clippings on the kidnapping. No telling why he saved them." Annie rotated her shoulders and tipped her head back and forth. "Maybe you were right about him, and our time would be better spent exploring other leads."

"What about the necklace?" Cole asked. Although he hadn't shared her enthusiasm for the Lockhart lead, he hated seeing it fizzle.

She shrugged and the neckline of her robe gaped open, giving him a glimpse of the shadows between her breasts. "Maybe the necklace was a gift for some woman and he was going to get it repaired," she suggested, absently fingering her lapel while Cole tried his best to stay focused. "Considering how flimsy the lock on his door is, I can't say I'd blame him for hiding it." She sounded discouraged.

"Are you all right?" Needing the contact with her, he covered her hand with his. Her skin was cool to the touch, and he couldn't resist caressing it with his fingertips.

"I'm tired," she replied without meeting his gaze, but at least she didn't pull away. "It's been a long day."

"Then come to bed with me," he invited.

She studied his face while he held his breath. They both knew what he was suggesting, and it wasn't sharing the bed for the sake of convenience. She didn't have the will to say no.

"All right." She got to her feet and then she didn't seem to know what to do. Cole circled the table and came up behind her. First he reached his arms around her waist and untied her belt, pressing close and wondering if she could feel how much he wanted her. When she didn't pull away, he slid the robe from her shoulders. His hands were trembling like a boy's.

Slowly Annie turned to face him, while Cole held his breath. She was so lovely that he thought his heart might stop beating.

"I wouldn't have dreamed it was possible, but you've grown even more beautiful," he said, surprised at how easily the compliment came to him. He didn't think of himself as a romantic man, but Annie brought out a side of him he'd nearly forgotten. It was a side he wasn't totally comfortable with, a vulnerable side.

"Thank you," she murmured as he brought her hand to his mouth and kissed it. Her gaze on his, she lifted her free hand and stroked his chest, sending a shiver of awareness through him. Passion swirled in her eyes, clouding them, and she swayed toward him. With a low groan, Cole caught her up in his arms and headed for the bed.

Annie woke up slowly, becoming aware by degrees that she was curled against a warm male body and that they were both naked. She wasn't a morning person, and it took another moment for her to remember what had taken place before sleep claimed her the night before.

Morning light bled through the curtains and illuminated the room. If Cole wasn't already awake, he soon would be. Annie eased herself away from him, and then she froze as his arm tightened, holding her fast. Damn him, he'd always been one of those people who woke instantly, while she stumbled around blinking and rubbing her eyes. It had never failed to amuse him, while annoying her.

Lying perfectly still, Annie debated what to do. Was he awake, or did she still have a chance to escape? Before she could decide, he solved the problem for her by lifting his head and looking at her in the dimness.

"Hi." His eyes were wary and the lower half of his face was blurred with whiskers. He looked so sweetly vulnerable that her heart turned over. All she wanted was to stay where she was.

Instead she escaped from beneath his arm and sat up, holding the sheet against her naked breasts. "I'm sorry," she muttered, cheeks burning. "I didn't mean to crowd you."

A gleam of amusement appeared in the depths of his eyes and the corner of his mouth lifted. Was he remembering too, how they always used to wake up with the covers falling off her side of the bed?

"Apology accepted," he said gravely.

Before she could think of a retort, he climbed out of bed, wearing nothing but a great tan, and headed

for the bathroom. Helplessly, Annie admired the
sweep of his bare back and compact rear until the
door shut behind him. With a sigh she lay back
down, trying to figure out how to handle the situation when he came back out.

Before he reappeared, she grabbed her robe and
slipped into it. When the bathroom door opened, she
watched him cross the room without a shred of discomfort.

"My turn," she said hastily, before he could
reach for her.

She was halfway to the bathroom when, without
warning, his pillow smacked her in the back of the
head. His self-satisfied chuckle goaded her like a red
flag. Without stopping to consider the consequences,
she whirled around, picked up the pillow and pelted
it back at him.

The loose sleeves of her robe hindered her aim;
the pillow hit the edge of the mattress and fell harm-
lessly to the floor. With a shout, Cole lunged for it
and missed. When he nearly tumbled out of bed, it
was Annie's turn to laugh. Before she thought to
retreat, he grabbed another fluffy weapon and ad-
vanced with a pathetic attempt at a menacing scowl.

Where had this playful streak come from? she
wondered as they circled each other warily. He'd
had too much dignity to stoop to such antics before,
but she couldn't disapprove of this new side to him.

"You don't scare me," she exclaimed, puckering
up to blow him a smacking kiss and then grabbing

an embroidered cushion from the chair. As she swung it, Cole pivoted to the side like a quarterback eluding a tackle. He tossed another pillow that she barely managed to dodge, all the while laughing helplessly. She stuck out her tongue and he rushed her with a shout of triumph, but she managed to swing the cushion again and smack him in the side of the head. He staggered. Then, to her dismay, he let out a *whoop* and tackled her.

Together they tumbled to the sheepskin rug as Annie shrieked a protest. Right before they landed, Cole twisted so she was on top and he took the brunt of the fall. His arms were like steel bands as she stared down at him, chest heaving. The laughter faded from his face and his hand cupped her head.

Desire swept through her. But a moment later her sense of self-preservation kicked in and she stiffened. "It's time we got going."

Instantly his expression changed from triumph to concern, and he let her go. Knees shaking with reaction, she scrambled to her feet. How could she explain or even admit that she felt as though she were being swallowed whole?

The awkwardness between them lasted through their meeting with their hosts. After he'd served them both coffee, Glen Appleberry apologized to Annie again and tore up the bill for their stay. In return, she assured the Appleberrys she had no intention of suing the Circle A.

"Mr. Lockhart left last night," Glen told them as

he escorted them from his office. "But you can't go without a good ranch breakfast under your belts. It's the only way Myrtle and I will really know there are no hard feelings over what happened."

Annie and Cole exchanged glances. He shrugged. It seemed easier not to argue with their host. When they entered the dining room, the couple they'd met the day before waved them over. Judging from the interested stares of the other guests, word of their confrontation with one of the employees had gotten around.

Annie tensed as Cole held out her chair, fearing an inquisition. Instead, after Carol Best asked whether Annie was okay, nothing more was said. Gradually, as the heaping plates of eggs, bacon, sausage and fried potatoes were served, the others at the table all started eating, and Annie began to relax. Beside her, Cole helped himself to the dish of fresh fruit that was passed.

As soon as he and Annie were done eating, they said goodbye to the other couple and left the dining hall. Cole returned Myrtle Appleberry's wave and then opened the car door for Annie without a word. Their bags were already in the trunk. As they drove through the gate, she couldn't resist one last backward glance. So much had happened in the last day and a half; she needed time to sort it out.

Meanwhile, Lily's case would keep her busy and there was still a chance that either the necklace or the pawn ticket from Lockhart's room might link him to Sophia. As soon as they got back to San Antonio, Annie intended to develop a few new leads.

As Cole drove in silence, she looked out the side window. Although the low-growing cedar and oak gave the impression of greenery, the ground in the Hill Country was actually quite rocky. Scattered among the chunks of limestone were prickly pear and other kinds of cactus. Perhaps Annie would explore the area at greater length someday when doing so wouldn't be too painful a reminder of the time she'd spent here with Cole.

According to the flyers she'd picked up in the lobby at the guest ranch, there were several tourist attractions in the area, including the LBJ State and National Historical Parks, a couple of museums and numerous places to eat. Annie hadn't been up this way for several years and a trip back someday might be pleasant.

"Share your thoughts?" Cole asked when several more miles had gone by.

"Just thinking about the case," Annie replied. "When I talked to Rosita, she mentioned a dream she'd had."

"Ryan says she's psychic," Cole replied in a cynical tone.

"I take it you don't believe in that."

"I heard about her dream." He rolled his eyes. "Something about horses and a trail of blood."

"And a pair of gloves," Annie added.

Cole glanced at her. "So?"

"Although the police found a lot of fingerprints in Sophia's suite, none of them were Lily's. What if the killer wore gloves?"

Cole arched a brow. "What are you getting at?"

"Lockhart wore leather work gloves both times I saw him." She shifted in her seat, crossing her legs. "I think it's time to take a closer look at his alibi."

"I thought you already questioned everyone at the ranch." Cole said.

"I'm curious about that call he received just at the right time to establish his presence at the bunkhouse. It's a little too convenient, if you ask me. Did you remember seeing any phone records with the police reports?"

"No, but I requested them, and I'll check again as soon as I get to the office." Cole slowed for a turn. "Now that Lockhart's unemployed and probably upset about getting fired, things could be getting dangerous. From here on, I want you to keep me apprised of every move you make."

"I don't think that's necessary," Annie protested.

Cole's expression was grim. "But *I* do. If you won't agree, I'll insist that Ryan fire you for your own safety."

Annie sat up straighter. "You wouldn't!"

"Watch me," Cole told her. "And you know I could do it. No matter how Ryan feels about clearing Lily, he would never sacrifice someone else to save her. He's not that kind of man."

Annie was too frustrated to reply. Instead she tried to come up with an argument to dissuade Cole from speaking to Ryan. How humiliating it would be if he did!

"I want your word that you'll keep me posted and that you won't take chances without talking to me first," Cole insisted.

"You're tying my hands," Annie cried. "I can't work like that."

"Yes, you can. As long as Lockhart is a suspect, we have to be careful. If he finds out you're an investigator, there's no telling what he might do."

Annie let out a sigh of annoyance. She had no doubt that Ryan would go along with Cole if he carried out his threat. "We don't know where Lockhart's gone," she pointed out. "And we don't have the time to find him."

"You're right," Cole conceded, "but I still want you to be careful."

"I should just quit," she grumbled. "You're impossible to work with."

His grin was smug. "I'm great to work with, and you're not a quitter."

She was about to tell him that he, on the other hand, was—but she didn't want to open up that particular can of worms now. Somehow she had to keep their personal relationship separate from the case, or Lily would be the one to suffer.

"All right," she said ungraciously. "And I'm serving notice right now that my next steps are go-

ing to be getting the photos of that necklace developed and checking out the pawnshop that ticket
came from. Do you want to go with me when I drop
off the film, or do you trust me to handle it on my
own?''

"I'm more worried about the pawnshop," Cole
replied, ignoring her sarcasm. ''What if you run into
Lockhart there? He may have noticed by now that
the ticket's missing.''

"Oh, gee, I'll look around before I go barging
in," Annie said, and now there was no mistaking
her sarcasm.

Color crept up Cole's jaw, making her slightly
ashamed of her outburst. Perhaps she should be flattered that he cared enough to worry.

"I'm sorry," she muttered. "It's just the case."

"I know." His voice was soft. Of course he
knew. It was his mother they were trying to save.

Cole turned on the radio and soft classical music
filled the car.

"I want to tell Ryan about those clippings you
found," he said. "It seems odd that Lockhart would
have them.''

"Both his sisters married into the Fortune family," Annie reminded him. "Maybe he's just concerned, but I agree that there could be something
more to it.''

"Yeah," Cole replied, and it was his turn to be
sarcastic. "Maybe Lockhart is really a bighearted

softie who's worried about a helpless baby and couldn't possibly murder anyone, even in a rage.''

There wasn't anything to say to that, so Annie remained silent. After a few minutes, Cole cleared his throat, and she noticed that his knuckles had paled on the steering wheel, as though he were gripping it too tightly.

"Where do we go from here?" he asked.

"I told you," Annie replied impatiently. "I'm going to get the film developed—"

Cole glanced at her briefly before he returned his attention to the road. "I'm not talking about the case."

"That's all we need to discuss," she said quickly. No way was she ready to talk about what had happened back in that room, not until she'd sorted it out in her own head.

"You can deny it all you want, but something important happened between us back there, and I think we need to discuss it," he said.

"Isn't it supposed to be women who like to analyze a situation afterward, not men?" Annie grumbled, digging her sunglasses out of her bag and putting them on. Maybe it was superficial, but she felt like she needed the protection. "Perhaps sleeping together again was inevitable."

It was Cole's turn to shake his head in denial. "If you're saying it happened because we were sharing a room—"

"I'm saying it happened because we share a history and we were probably both curious."

Cole swore under his breath. "That was a hell of a lot of mighty damn combustible curiosity in that room. When are you going to face the fact that there's still something between us?"

Annie turned to stare out the side window. "Never," she said firmly. "Whatever was between us ended a long time ago. That was all the closure I needed."

"Then how do you explain what happened?" he asked.

"Did you ever think you might have been scratching an itch caused by someone else?" she blurted, trying to distract him.

"Not for a second," he replied. "You haven't changed that much, honey, and Lockhart's not your type."

"I suppose you are?" she demanded. Talk about ego!

He was so silent that she couldn't resist the urge to look at him.

"I used to be," he said then.

"And we know how that ended." Annie could hear the bitterness in her own voice and it made her cringe. What if he figured out she was still as besotted with him as ever? She'd die of shame.

"I heard the charges were dropped against you," he said, throwing her off with the abrupt change of subject. "I was glad for you."

"Thank you," she managed in a chilly voice.

"Good thing your partner finally admitted you weren't a part of the bribery scheme."

Annie didn't say anything. What was the use after all this time? It wasn't a part of her life she liked to think about.

"Why didn't you explain that your partner was the guilty one when I asked you?" He slowed to take a turn, his hands skillful on the wheel of the Lexus.

"Would you have believed me if I had?" she shot back. "I didn't have any proof, only my word."

"Your word would have been good enough for me," he insisted. "It was your refusal to tell me anything that I couldn't deal with."

Oh, no, she wasn't about to let him get away with that. "You might have convinced yourself, but I knew you. You're an attorney. I knew the way that orderly, analytical, tidy mind of yours worked. You would have pelted me with questions that I couldn't answer."

"And why not?" Cole demanded, hurt creeping into his voice. "We were lovers. Were you afraid to confide in me?"

"I *couldn't* talk to you or to anyone," Annie said, all the frustration she'd felt at the time coming back in a rush. Her father had told her, over and over, *Annie, you don't rat on a fellow cop.* "Les was my partner," she said.

Cole shook his head in disgust. "And you

couldn't betray your partner, even though he betrayed you.''

"That's right," she agreed hotly. "I couldn't break the code of silence. Besides, in the end Les did the right thing, admitting that I didn't have any idea what he and a few others were up to.''

"Yeah, I heard he finally came clean when Internal Affairs had their case against him nailed shut. Took his time about it.''

"He couldn't say anything without incriminating himself or the others who were involved. *He* was hampered by the code of silence too. After I.A. completed their investigation, it no longer mattered.'' She'd understood the system. She hadn't liked it, but had no choice but to go along with it. The whole experience had soured her for police work, though. Even now, the memory of how scared and alone she'd felt were enough to make her shiver.

"What good did that code of silence do you?'' Cole asked. "You still left the force.''

Annie pushed her sunglasses back up her nose and wrapped a strand of hair around her finger. "I left with my honor intact,'' she said softly. "Maybe it's hard for you to understand, but ratting on Les would have dishonored my father as well as myself.'' He'd never asked if she was guilty, and she hadn't said, not even to him. "I couldn't do that, but once I was cleared, I realized I no longer wanted to be part of it. I left on my own terms.''

How disappointed her father had been when she

quit. *Annie, you don't know what you're doing,* he'd said. *Give it time. You'll feel differently.* Until the day he died, he'd never understood why she left, but she liked to think he'd eventually been proud of what she accomplished. He'd never said, so she didn't know for sure.

"Ryan told me about your father," Cole said bluntly. "I'm sorry. Was it his heart?"

"A stroke," Annie replied. "The doctors said he probably never knew what hit him." Not being able to say goodbye had been painful for her. Since she was small her father had raised her alone, and being a single parent with a cop's schedule couldn't have been easy. Despite Cole's obvious family problems, she envied him his relationship with his mother.

"Would you actually have taken the fall with Gordon?" he asked. "Gone to jail if it came to that?"

Annie bowed her head and stared at her clenched hands. "I don't honestly know," she admitted, "but I'm glad I didn't have to find out."

Cole shook his head. "I guess I just don't get that kind of blind loyalty."

"No kidding," Annie couldn't help but retort. "You didn't have much loyalty toward me at the time."

"I didn't know what to think!" he retorted. "You wouldn't talk to me."

"I thought you'd know I was innocent," she cried, the pain pressing down on her chest. "I was a good cop. How could you ever think I'd do something so dishonest?''

It was Cole's turn to glance away. They'd loved each other. Was he thinking about all they'd lost because of something neither of them could control. "I needed to hear it from you," he admitted. "I'm sorry."

Annie appeared surprised, he noticed. At the time he hadn't understood the pressure she must have felt to honor that stupid code. There had to be some way to convince her to forget the past and enjoy what they had now. But if there was, he sure didn't know what it might be. Maybe after the trial was over and before he went back to Denver, he could figure out how to make things right between them.

"Are you sure you don't remember seeing it on Sophie?" Annie asked Ryan the next afternoon as she showed him the photo she'd had developed of the necklace she found hidden in Lockhart's boot. They were standing with Cole in the living room at the ranch, and Rosita had just gone upstairs to fetch Lily.

Ryan shook his head. "Sophia had a lot of jewelry," he said regretfully, "and sometimes I didn't even recognize what I bought her myself, but I sure don't remember this." He looked at Annie. "Maybe it wasn't hers."

"Maybe not." She tried not to let her frustration show. It would have been nice to link Lockhart with

Sophia. She was running out of ideas. "What about this?" she asked, sliding the gold watch she'd redeemed at the pawnshop from an envelope and holding it out. "Did you ever notice Lockhart wearing anything like this?" She'd been disappointed when she first saw what it was, had been hoping instead that the ticket might be for something more damning.

She'd questioned the pawnshop owner about Lockhart, but he claimed not to remember anything, even when she offered him a little incentive. It had cost her a twenty just to find out he didn't think Lockhart had been in before the one time he'd pawned the watch.

Now Ryan picked it up between two fingers, frowning, and turned it over. "It's not a brand I recognize and it doesn't have the weight of a quality piece. This is like Lockhart himself, just a cheap copy of something with value. But I don't remember him wearing it. Sorry, I wish I could be more help." There was frustration in Ryan's voice.

"Has anyone at the bunkhouse complained of anything turning up missing over the last few months?" Annie asked.

Ryan's frown cleared. "I'll find out. You think he stole it?"

"I don't know," she said thoughtfully, "but if he pawned it, he must have been low on funds. Before he left here so abruptly he bragged that a woman friend was coming into a lot of money. Then Sophia gets herself killed, and suddenly Lockhart is pawning things.''

"So why didn't he pawn that necklace?" Cole asked.

"Because he thought it might be traced?" Annie shrugged. "I'm no expert, but that necklace appeared to be a lot more valuable than this watch."

Footsteps sounded above them, and Annie looked up to see Lily descending the staircase with Rosita trailing behind her. Like the rest of them, Lily was wearing jeans. Her coral tank top matched her bright lipstick and revealed her tanned, shapely arms. It wasn't until she joined them that Annie noticed the lines of strain bracketing her mouth.

"I'm sorry I kept you waiting," she said as Ryan slipped his arm around her shoulders. "I was taking a nap."

"Did you get any rest?" he asked.

She managed a smile. "A little."

As soon as she and Annie exchanged greetings, Annie showed her and Rosita the watch and the photo. "Do you recognize either of these?"

She held her breath while they both studied the watch. "This could be anyone's," Lily said, handing it back. "I know men who wear gold watches, but there's nothing about this one that stands out." Then she looked at the picture of the necklace. "I think Sophia had one like this." She tapped it with her finger.

"Are you sure?" Annie asked.

"Pretty sure. At least it was similar."

Rosita frowned. "I don't know. It could have been hers."

Lily handed back the photo. "Where did you get this?"

"I found the necklace in Lockhart's possession." Annie was relieved when neither Lily nor Ryan asked for details. "As you can see from the picture, it has a broken chain."

"What does it mean?" Lily asked, obviously puzzled.

"It means if the necklace did belong to Sophia, he knew her better than we realized," Cole told her. "He could be the one who was feeding her information about you and Ryan. It's even possible the necklace broke when they were struggling."

Lily glanced from him to Annie and back. "Do you think he's the one who killed her?" Her voice was breathless, as if her throat had closed.

Annie could imagine how she might feel. She laid her hand on the older woman's arm. "It's a possibility," she said softly. "Unfortunately nothing we found is admissible in court."

Lily's elation faded. "But why not?"

"There are rules of evidence that we didn't exactly follow," Cole explained. "But it may point to something else. In the meantime, we have some other leads to explore."

"You're doing a great job," Ryan exclaimed.

"Thank you, both!" After a couple more minutes of conversation, he invited Annie to stay for dinner.

"I can't," she said reluctantly. "Cole and I have some paperwork to go over back in town, don't we?" She looked at him expectantly.

"Yes, we do," he replied. "My secretary left a message on my cell phone. Those records I requested came by messenger."

"Records?" Ryan asked.

"Phone records. Just a few more puzzle pieces that need looking into," Cole replied smoothly. "We'll keep you posted."

After kissing his mother's cheek, he placed his hand on the small of Annie's back. "I'll follow you into town."

When she bade the two older people goodbye, there was a speculative expression on Lily's face. Could she somehow tell that Annie had slept with her son? A mother's intuition didn't extend *that* far, did it?

"You two run along," Lily said, her voice lighter. "And make Cole buy you a nice dinner somewhere. You've certainly earned it. And he's on an expense account."

Nine

When Cole pushed open the door to his office and gestured for Annie to go on in, he was still pondering his mother's awkward comment. Had there been some special reason behind her suggestion that he take Annie to dinner?

He watched as she sat down and crossed her legs. She didn't look as though she was starving. Instead, her feminine curves threatened to distract him from the business at hand.

"Mr. Cassidy?" Tiffany handed him the records that had arrived by messenger and several pink phone memos. As he went into his office, he glanced through them. One was from his sister Hannah, but none appeared urgent. She probably wanted to know if he'd contacted Maria yet. Damn, with everything else that had happened, he'd forgotten all about running down his pain-in-the-butt baby sister.

Shutting the door behind him, he dropped the stack of messages by his phone and sat down next to Annie. With little success he tried to ignore her scent and the way her hair beckoned him to rub its silken strands between his fingers. He used to love the feel of it sliding over his bare skin.

With a sigh, he spread out the records. "Maybe these will tell us something," he said, hoping the call to the bunkhouse on the night of the murder wasn't another dead end.

"Let's hope so." Annie skimmed down the list he handed her with her finger. It didn't take long to find the entry they wanted. "Look at this," she said, pointing.

After he'd absorbed the information, Cole sat back in his chair and blew out a long breath. "What a coincidence," he murmured with a touch of irony. "The call that established Lockhart's alibi just happened to be made from the parking garage of the Austin Arms Hotel, where Sophia was killed." Maybe Annie had been right about Lockhart all along.

"Interesting," she murmured.

Cole sifted through the possibilities. "Maybe Flynn lied about Lockhart being in his room at the bunkhouse, and Lockhart called himself to establish his alibi or someone else called Lockhart from the hotel."

"An accomplice?" Annie asked. "Letting Lockhart know Sophia had been taken care of? That suggests premeditation. But why?"

It was Cole's turn to frown as he struggled to make sense of the new information. It put either Lockhart or someone he knew at the scene of the crime, but what did it all mean? "You're right. If Lockhart had an accomplice, the murder had to have been planned."

Annie's eyes widened and then she pursed her lips thoughtfully. Distracted, Cole quelled the impulse to get up and pull her into his arms. Since they'd been together at the Circle A, he couldn't stop thinking about her. Wanting her. Right in the middle of a murder investigation. If she didn't appear to be so focused on business, he might kiss her, distracting them both until they forgot why they were here.

Not a good idea, under the circumstances.

"You think Lockhart established an alibi because he *planned* to kill Sophia?" she asked, oblivious to his inner struggle. "That doesn't make any sense. If she was the woman he bragged was coming into money, why kill the golden goose?"

Absently, Cole ran his fingers up and down the lapel of his suit coat. What could have happened between Sophia and Clint? A partnership gone sour?

"What if they had something to do with Bryan's kidnapping?" he asked.

Annie nodded. "That's certainly one possibility." Was Ryan's wife crazy and bitter enough to get mixed up in that kind of thing?

"But why would she risk going to prison for kidnapping when all she had to do was bleed Ryan for a fat settlement?" Annie asked. "I don't think she'd take that chance."

"I suppose you're right." There had to be a more

logical reason for her murder. "What if Sophia had promised Lockhart a share of what she got from Ryan in the divorce settlement in payment for spying?" he mused. "Perhaps she tried to cut him out of the action. Or she took up with someone else, or he got tired of waiting for the money." He drummed his fingers on the edge of the desk. "Perhaps he didn't plan on killing her at all, but set up the alibi for some other reason."

"Like what?" Absently Annie curled a strand of hair around her finger.

Cole wondered if she had any idea how provocative the gesture was. "I doubt he would want Ryan to know he was involved with her, especially if he was Sophia's pipeline to inside information. What if Lockhart was worried that someone might see him with her at the hotel, and tell Ryan? This way, if it ever came up, Lockhart's got an alibi."

Cole nearly groaned aloud when Annie nibbled her lip thoughtfully. "It sounds pretty far-fetched, but I'd sure love to ask him about it."

The last thing Cole wanted was for her to be anywhere near Lockhart, especially if he was a killer. "Except that we don't know where he went after he left the Circle A," he pointed out.

"True. I guess it's time for you to call the D.A.'s office with this information. Maybe they can find him."

"When it comes to considering anyone besides my mother for this murder, the authorities are wear-

ing blinders.'' Cole didn't even try to keep the bitterness from his voice. ''I'll alert them to what we
found about the phone call, but I doubt they'd be
willing to bother with Lockhart at this point. Even
without him, we can raise a few doubts in the minds
of the jury, if the case gets that far.''

''You think it might not?'' Annie asked.

Cole struggled to remain practical, despite the elation that was starting to form inside him like a big
bubble. The state's case, shaky to start with, was
getting weaker. ''Who knows how far they'll take
it. We need to find more chinks in the state's ar-
mor.''

What he said made sense to Annie. While he was
preparing his case for court, she would explore a
few other avenues, all the while hoping she could
pick up Lockhart's trail again. ''I have a friend
who's good at locating people,'' she said as she tried
to ignore her own immediate reaction to Cole's
smile. ''I'll give him a call, and then I'll get to
work.''

''What's next?'' Cole asked.

''It's time to revisit the scene of the crime. I'm
going back to the hotel.'' There were still a few
rocks left unturned.

''What do you hope to find there?'' he asked.

Annie shrugged. ''Maybe someone saw who
made that call from the garage. One of the maids
on Sophia's floor has been out sick, but she's back

to work—I'd like to talk to her too. Oh, what are you doing?''

Cole had gotten to his feet. Now he cupped her elbows and drew her up with him. His nearness made her pulse rate shoot into the stratosphere. ''I think I should go with you to the Austin Arms,'' he murmured, his mouth hovering near hers.

Annie could feel herself start to melt in reaction to the intense interest in his bright gaze. Giving in to temptation, she reached up to run a finger down his cheek, fascinated by the way his pupils expanded in response. ''Why is that?''

''Unlike some places, we don't have to pretend to be married to share a room.'' His voice was husky. ''Do you think our investigation will take more than one day?''

Annie knew when this was over he'd go back to Denver and she would be left once again to pick up the pieces of her life. So who could blame her for grabbing this opportunity? Being with Cole wouldn't interfere with the investigation. She wouldn't let it. But it would give her one more memory to savor.

Deliberately she leaned back in his embrace and moistened her lips with her tongue. ''I'm sure we'll have to spend the night in Austin.'' She circled her arms around his neck. His gaze was fixed on her mouth, eyes narrowed. ''Investigating can be such a dirty job,'' she added with a pout.

''Then I'd better tell Tiffany to make a reservation." Instead of reaching for the intercom, he lowered his head with agonizing slowness.

His lips finally settled on hers, nibbling gently. As Annie responded with helpless abandon, he changed the angle of the kiss. Clinging to him, she joined him in the wild, restless ride, the floor shifting beneath her feet as she opened her mouth and met his passion head-on. Her mind blurred and she forgot where they were, forgot to think at all.

Vaguely she heard a knock on the office door, and then abruptly it opened. Annie sprang back, dropping her arms, but not quite soon enough.

As Cole's secretary poked her head through the doorway, her bland expression never altered. "Your sister Hannah's on the phone," she told Cole. "You didn't say to hold your calls. Shall I tell her you'll get back to her?"

Cole glanced at the phone on his desk with a frown. "There was a message from Hannah in that stack. Perhaps I'd better take the call."

The mood was broken, and Annie had plenty of work to do. She glanced at her watch. "I'm meeting a girlfriend for dinner tonight, so I'll talk to you later."

"Shall we head for Austin tomorrow?" he asked.

How she wished they didn't have to wait, but she couldn't cancel on Lydia. They'd gone through the police academy together and still met for lunch or dinner every couple of months.

"Tomorrow would be fine," she said, hoping he couldn't guess at her thoughts.

Cole's glance slid to her mouth, his eyes dark, and she realized she wasn't the only one anticipating their trip. She wished Tiffany would leave so he could kiss her again, but apparently his assistant was waiting to be dismissed.

Cole reached for the phone. "Okay," he said absently. His mind was clearly on his sister.

Wait until tomorrow, Annie promised him silently as she picked up her bag from the floor. Only when she walked out the door did she make eye contact with his secretary, whose lips quirked into a contrite smile.

"Sorry for the interruption," she whispered.

Annie was tempted to reply that Tiffany couldn't be half as sorry as Annie herself was. "No problem," she said as she kept walking.

After she left and Tiffany closed the door to Cole's office behind her, he gave in to an impulse. There was a call he wanted to make as soon as he talked to Hannah. He picked up the receiver, admitting to Hannah he hadn't yet bothered to contact Maria.

"I'm not ready to bury the hatchet yet," Hannah told him, "or I'd go call her myself."

Cole scribbled a note on his pad. "I'm going to be out of town for a day or so," he replied. "I'll go to Leather Bucket when I get back."

"Does it have to do with Mom's case?" she asked.

"Not entirely." As soon as the words were out, he wished he could recall them. "I'm going to Austin with Annie Jones," he admitted, making the situation even worse.

"Didn't you just get back from that guest ranch with her?" Hannah asked.

"That's right."

There was a silence. He doubted Hannah would remember that he'd once been seeing someone named Annie.

"Are you attracted to this woman?" Hannah asked.

Over the years, Cole had confided in his sister on more than one occasion, so her question didn't surprise him.

"You know I wouldn't jeopardize the investigation," he felt compelled to say.

Hannah wasn't the kind of person to pry. "I know that," she replied. "Have a good trip, and don't forget to get in touch with Maria."

"I won't." He'd barely ended the conversation and hung up the receiver when Tiffany put through a call from his mother.

He figured she was trying to determine whether he'd acted on her less-than-subtle suggestion that he take Annie to dinner. "I'm on my own this evening," he volunteered to save her the trouble of trying to worm the information out of him. "Annie had plans, so I'll probably grab a sandwich and do some paperwork. Better yet, why don't you drive into town, and I'll take you out?'' They needed to spend time together, to rediscover the easy affection they'd shared before Lily dropped her bombshell about his father.

"Why don't you quit work for the day and come out to the ranch instead?" she countered. "Rosita's fixing a beef roast. I was in the kitchen a little while ago and it smells wonderful. We'd have time for a visit before Ryan gets home for dinner, and then we can all eat together.''

She, too, must want to get past the awkwardness between them. If he couldn't be with Annie this evening, he could at least mend a few fences while he was enjoying a good meal.

"I'll leave now,'' Cole said. "See you soon.''

When Annie got back to her own office, she checked her fax machine, listened to her phone messages and went through her mail. It was mostly bills, along with a couple of credit card offers, several ads and a catalog for surveillance equipment. She flipped through the pages in a pathetic attempt to keep her thoughts from straying in dangerous directions, but to little avail.

At least this time around she knew Cole would be leaving. It might be too late to spare her heart, but she had no one but herself to blame for making the same mistake twice. She'd known going in that they had no future together, but her attraction toward him had been too strong to resist.

She was staring at a page of tiny video cameras, trying unsuccessfully to concentrate, when the front door to her office opened.

"Annie Jones?" asked a deliveryman carrying a vase of flowers.

She gaped at the breathtaking arrangement of white roses, their partially unfurled petals edged with pink, and managed to bob her head. A couple of times grateful clients had sent flowers, but nothing like these.

"Where would you like them?" He glanced at her desk, covered with folders and papers, then did a slow perusal of the rest of her cluttered office.

"Give them to me." With trembling hands she set the vase on a manila folder while he took a clipboard from under his arm and extended it.

"Sign here, please."

Annie dashed off her signature and then she reached for her purse. "Just a moment."

"Oh, it's been taken care of," he replied before she could unearth her wallet. "Have a nice day."

As soon as the man was gone, she sank into her chair and stared at the impressive bouquet. The long-stemmed blooms were nestled among leathery dark green leaves in a round crystal bowl trimmed with a satin bow in the same delicate pink as the roses. If this had been sent by a grateful client, she'd eat her denim tote bag.

With fingers that shook, and hope blooming in her heart, Annie plucked the small white envelope from its resting place among the leaves and opened it.

Tomorrow was written in a slash of black on the card, followed by the initials *C.C.* Grinning foolishly, Annie stared at the bold, familiar writing. Then she tucked the card back into its envelope and put it carefully in her purse for safekeeping. Turning the vase this way and that, she examined every one of the twelve roses. In her whole life, no one had ever given her flowers for a romantic reason.

Perhaps Cole sends them to every woman he sleeps with, whispered an insidious little voice. It was his kind of gesture: sophisticated, polished and charming.

No, she wouldn't think that way. She was going to savor the roses until they withered and died, just as she was going to enjoy Cole's company as long as he was in San Antonio. And afterward she'd get on with her life. Yes, the way to think of this time was definitely as an interlude. Nothing more.

She should thank Cole for the bouquet, she realized eventually, but when she called his office he'd already gone. She wasn't about to leave a message on his voice mail; she'd see him tomorrow.

Nor was she going to leave the roses on her desk to wilt while she was in Austin. If she hurried, she'd have just enough time to drop them off at her condo before she met Lydia for dinner. Otherwise her friend was sure to pepper her with questions for which Annie had no answers.

Driving to the ranch, Cole wondered if Annie had enjoyed his impulse. The florist had promised the roses would be delivered right away.

Perhaps Cole shouldn't have sent them. It had been his observation that romantic gestures could complicate an issue, but the situation between them was simple. Seeing each other had rekindled their desire for each other. What could be more straight-forward? Besides, he remembered how much she had always loved flowers. Funny, in the months they'd been together before, he didn't remember ever sending them.

When he pulled up in front of the ranch house and went inside, one of the maids showed him to the small, elegant sitting room his mother had re-decorated at Ryan's insistence. The rich jewel tones and antique cherry furniture she had chosen flattered her exotic coloring.

After Lily gave him a hug, the familiar scent of her perfume relaxing him as it always did, they sat side by side on a deep blue velvet couch that was as comfortable as it was attractive.

"Have you seen Maria lately?" Cole asked as she poured iced water with sliced lime from a silver pitcher into a crystal goblet and handed it to him. Perhaps he wouldn't have to drive to Leather Bucket, after all.

While he drank deeply, Lily shook her head with obvious regret. "I don't know what's going on with that girl. She finally called after I left several messages, but when I invited her over, she said she was busy." Lily bit her lip. "I worry about her," she said. "Something isn't right, but I can't put my finger on it."

As far as Cole was concerned, there was always plenty to worry about with Maria. She seemed to embrace trouble.

"Hannah suggested that I check on her." He was annoyed at the twinge of guilt he felt, despite his baby sister's complete lack of regard for her family. He didn't care how she treated him, but the way she tried to undermine their mother's happiness was despicable. He didn't understand why Lily tolerated it, and he wasn't looking forward to Maria finding out about his parentage. It would only make matters worse. "I haven't had time to drive out there," he said. Perhaps he wouldn't mention the trip to Austin.

His mother patted his hand. "You've been busy."

"I'll get over there one day soon," he promised. Maybe Annie would go with him. There was no telling how Maria would react to the intrusion. A third party might serve as a buffer against her volatile temper.

"I hope you can talk some sense into her." Lily took a deep breath, and he would have sworn she was bracing herself. Before she could speak, there was a soft knock on the partially closed door, and

Rosita came in with a tray. "Just put it on the coffee table," Lily said, and thanked her.

The tray held a small platter of fresh fruit, silverware, plates and napkins. "I thought you might like something to keep you going until dinner," Lily told Cole.

Realizing that he'd missed lunch, he helped himself to some melon and papaya. "How are you holding up?" he asked. "Have you been sleeping okay?"

"I'm fine. Ryan is very supportive." She twisted her engagement ring around her finger, then blurted, "Do you think we have a chance of winning this case?"

Cole froze in the act of spearing a slice of cantaloupe. Where was this coming from?

Carefully he set down his fork so he could give her his full attention. The tension she tried to hide was evident in the lines of strain between her dark brows and around her mouth, in the way she gripped her hands together in her lap so tightly that the knuckles paled.

Cole covered her hands with his, dismayed at how icy they felt. "The case is full of holes," he said. "If we can't win, I don't deserve to be called an attorney." He was gratified when the corners of her mouth softened slightly. "Believe me," he continued, releasing her to sit back on the couch, "I'm not just saying it to make you feel better. Annie's been working hard to undermine the pitiful amount of evidence the state's come up with. You have no reason to worry.''

Cole knew that until the verdict came in there were always reasons—unpredictable juries, bad rulings, uncooperative or forgetful witnesses, technical snafus—but he wasn't about to mention any of that to his mother. She needed reassurance, not more worries.

"Anything new on the kidnapping?" he asked to distract her.

"Technically the case is still open, but the police have run down every possible lead, and the investigators Ryan hired keep coming up empty as well.'' Tears filled her eyes, and Cole realized he'd picked a poor change of subject. "We can only pray the baby is still alive somewhere,'' she added. "Ryan clings to that hope.''

"Of course Bryan's alive,'' Cole replied. "And someday we'll find him.''

Lily sipped her water. "How is Annie?'' she asked. "She seems like such a nice girl.''

Her smile relieved Cole, so he didn't pay as much attention as he might have to the hairs lifting in warning on the back of his neck. "She's stubborn, she's opinionated and she's too independent for her own good,'' he said without thinking as he selected a chunk of fresh pineapple. "Other than that, I guess she's fine.''

He glanced up to see that his mother's expression

had brightened even more. Too late he realized he'd admitted way too much.

"Has she changed a lot since you knew her before?"

"Before?" Cole echoed, ice sliding down his spine.

"Before you moved away, when you two were seeing each other romantically."

He didn't need the clarification. "I didn't realize you knew about that." He concentrated on trimming the rind from a slice of cantaloupe as though he were performing major surgery.

"Mothers are good at that kind of math," she replied dryly. "Adding two and two, getting four. I thought her name sounded familiar, so I asked her."

Oh, Lord, how much had Annie revealed? He wasn't proud of the way he'd treated her. Looking back on it, he realized he could have handled the situation better than he had, but he'd been too damn devastated at the time to think clearly.

"I tried to help her," he said now, "but she wouldn't listen. How was I supposed to know she was innocent when she wouldn't even defend herself?"

"Why don't you tell me what happened," Lily suggested, folding her hands and arousing Cole's suspicion. Just how much did she already know, or how little?

Briefly, he explained how Annie's partner on the

San Antonio police force had been on the take, and
that Annie had been implicated too.

"You loved her, but you believed she was
guilty?" Lily sounded incredulous.

"She wouldn't explain," Cole replied defensively. "She refused to answer my questions. Instead she kept insisting that she couldn't talk about
it." He waved his fork. "The evidence against her
was pretty damning. How was I supposed to know
what to think?"

Lily sat back and stared at him. "I've heard of
the loyalty among police officers. It sounds like she
had no choice in following her conscience, reasonable or not, but she needed your unconditional support all the same. How terribly hurt she must have
been that you couldn't give it."

He didn't know what to say. All this time, he'd
focused on his own frustration and his sense of betrayal. Now his mother's simple statement brought
home how much he'd let Annie down too.

"My God," he muttered beneath his breath. "I
never thought of it that way. I didn't really listen. I
didn't understand. Maybe I was too busy thinking
about *my* needs, *my* hurt. I let her down and then I
walked out on her."

Cole stared down at his fists, sick at heart. He
was lucky Annie hadn't shot him on sight that first
day in the restaurant.

"It was a long time ago," Lily said gently. "Perhaps it no longer matters."

His head snapped up. "It matters to me. I still—"
He stopped abruptly, swallowing hard on the emotions he wasn't yet ready to face. "I still care about
what Annie thinks," he amended. He had held her
and made love to her. They'd connected on the most
basic level.

"You don't understand," he said bluntly. "It's
six years too late to tell her I'm sorry. The attraction
might still be there, but the trust is gone."

"That's a shame," Lily said with obvious regret,
"but I can tell you from experience that trust can
be rebuilt, if you care enough and are willing to
forgive each other. Look at Ryan and me. For thirty
years I let him believe I'd stopped loving him."

"That's different," Cole argued. It was easy to
see that Ryan adored her. Annie might want Cole,
but neither one of them believed they could turn
back the clock. Except for a very few exceptions,
like his mother and Ryan, life didn't very often hand
out second chances.

"If you say so," Lily replied, but she didn't
sound convinced. It was time to change the subject
once again.

"She's going to talk to some of the employees at
the Austin Arms again tomorrow," he said.

"The police already interviewed everyone who
was working that night," Lily protested. "What
does she hope to find?"

"I'm not sure," Cole admitted. "That's Annie's

field of expertise. All I know is that she seemed to be looking forward to the trip.''

So was he. In fact, he couldn't remember the last time he'd looked forward to anything quite as much.

Ten

Nothing about the Austin Arms had changed since the last time Annie had been here, and yet everything was different. Cole's light touch on her back as he followed her to the elevator and up to their room burned through her cotton sweater like a branding iron. The pep talk she'd given herself on the way here—something about living for the moment and letting the future take care of itself—had been as effective as a rain dance in the desert.

She could deny the shouting of her heart no longer. She loved Cole, had always loved him. And worse, would probably keep loving him until she died.

Silently she unlocked the door to their room and was about to step inside when he stopped her. Annie's overnight bag was slung over his shoulder and he was carrying a small case of his own, which he set down on the patterned carpet of the hallway.

"What?" she asked in confusion, gripping her purse and tote bag more tightly. "This is our room. The key worked."

Cole settled his hands lightly on her shoulders.

His smile was crooked, his eyes a dark and intense blue. As always, his appearance sent a sizzle of desire through her veins.

When he'd picked her up at her condo, she had thanked him for the roses sitting on her dining room table. Despite the awareness crackling between them, their conversation since then had been strictly business as they discussed every aspect of the case in exhaustive detail. Cole's witness list was shaping up nicely and he was encouraged.

Now his expression was anything but professional as he searched Annie's face. Her heart began to thump wildly, and she barely resisted the urge to fiddle with her hair. She'd worn it down today instead of in its usual ponytail, since Cole had mentioned how much he liked it loose. It made her feel feminine and flirtatious.

"I know we have the right room," he agreed. His voice was deeper than usual, his expression almost predatory in its intensity. "Annie—" he started, and then stopped to clear his throat. "I'm glad we're here together," he said simply.

Another door opened down the hall and a man came out. As he walked by, he glanced at them indifferently. Cole lifted his hands from her shoulders and picked up his bag.

Intensely curious about what he'd been about to say, Annie led the way inside. Her feet sank into the thick blue carpet with every step. A huge bed dominated the room. Trying to ignore it, she set down her purse and crossed to the window to open the heavy draperies. The sky had been cloudy when they left San Antonio, and now a gentle rain was falling.

Her senses were more keenly tuned to Cole moving around behind her than to the view. She would have given a lot to know what he was thinking, how he was feeling. With the new information about Lockhart's alibi and the lack of evidence against his mother, there was an excellent chance that Lily would be vindicated.

Annie knew a chance wasn't good enough for Cole. He wanted a guarantee, and the only way they would have that was to find out the identity of the real killer. That's why they were here in Austin.

That was *one* reason, she amended as his arms slid around her from behind. She leaned back against him, tipping her head. With a sigh he nuzzled the side of her neck, his breath warm against her skin. Every cell in Annie's being responded with an ache that would have buckled her knees had he not been holding her.

"Work before play," she gasped as she covered his hands with her own to stop their slow ascent up her rib cage.

Cole made a sound of disappointment. "You're right," he said with a gusty sigh. "Where do we start?"

Ducking around him, Annie unsnapped her denim tote and pulled out a manila folder. "I want to talk to the maid I mentioned before and to the garage

attendant who was on duty that night," she said,
studying her notes. "I already checked. As luck
would have it, they're both working today."

"What can I do?" Cole asked.

She took out two copies of the photo of Lockhart
and handed one to him. Briefly they discussed a plan
of action and decided to meet back at the room in
time for dinner. By unspoken agreement they were
both aware that the evening and the rest of the night
were reserved for the two of them.

When Cole disappeared into the bathroom, Annie
whipped a dress from her overnight bag and hung it
in the closet so it wouldn't wrinkle. By the time he
came back out, she had run a brush through her hair
and renewed her lip gloss.

"All set?" he asked, checking to make sure he
had a room key.

"I think so." Packing her notes, the photo and a
small tablet of paper into her bag, she resisted the
urge to move into his arms, and headed toward the
door instead. Silently, they rode the elevator back
down to the lobby.

"Happy hunting." As the doors slid open, he
merged with a cluster of people heading toward the
bar and his quarry. Annie continued down to the
parking garage and the pay phone she figured had
been used by the last person to see Sophia alive.

When Cole got back to the room later, the shower
was running and the bathroom door was closed.

Maybe Annie had been more successful in her quest than he had. He'd known when he started that the chance he'd uncover anything new at this point was slim, but it would have been nice to break the case wide open.

"I'm back," he called out when the shower went off. He hung his jacket over a chair and stripped off his shirt. Before he could take a fresh one off its hanger, the door opened and Annie peered through the crack, a towel wrapped around her like a toga.

"Any luck?" she asked.

"The trail is cold. How about you?"

"I'm afraid not. The maid didn't recognize Lockhart's picture, and the garage attendant couldn't remember who used the phone that night. He was too busy getting cars for the people from the banquet your mother attended. He did say that no one else has questioned him about it, though."

Cole shook his head angrily. "Of course not. The police had the ruby bracelet. What more proof did they need?"

"Your mother never should have been charged," Annie replied. "Perhaps you don't want to stay. Would you rather go back to San Antonio tonight?"

Cole was tempted to push the bathroom door open wider and peel her out of that towel, but he didn't want to make her nervous. He owed her a meal before he ravished her. And ravish her thoroughly he would.

"Of course I don't want to leave," he said with

what he hoped was a humor-filled grin. "I've heard the food here is good, and I'm looking forward to a nice, relaxing dinner. After that I'll be much too tired to drive, so I guess you're stuck here with me."

To his relief, Annie batted her eyes. "Then I'll just finish getting ready," she cooed.

After the door shut behind her, Cole flipped on the television to keep the image of her without that towel at bay. As he listened to the local news, he put on his shirt and knotted his tie. He thought about calling his mother, but he was reluctant to admit he was spending the night in Austin with Annie. Lily's imagination was fertile enough as it was, and he had no doubt she'd get the information out of him before he knew what he was saying.

Cole was watching a story about road rage on the freeway when he heard the latch *click* on the bathroom door. Glancing up, he nearly swallowed his tongue. Annie was poised in the doorway in a killer black dress that left her arms and a great deal of her shapely legs bare.

"Wow," he muttered, suddenly inarticulate. She was wearing black shoes with high heels and skinny rhinestone straps. The dress had a scoop neck and black beading that made it shimmer when she moved. Her hair was down, but she'd tucked it behind her ears to reveal glittery earrings. A matching pendant winked from the shadow between her breasts.

As she floated toward him with a smile of pure

lust, Cole struggled with the image of her wearing just the pendant and the earrings. Her eyes were smoky and her lips were painted kiss-me red. The scent teasing his nostrils whispered seduction, sending a zap of electricity through him that centered somewhere south of his belt buckle.

"You look fantastic," he managed without stuttering. Glad he'd followed his instincts, he reached for the package he'd picked up on his way back to the room, and handed it to her.

Annie's eyes widened when she saw the blood-red orchid in the clear plastic bubble. "More flowers," she exclaimed. "Thank you." Her smile widened. No doubt she was used to flowers from men, but Cole wanted her wearing his token tonight.

He eyed the skimpy bodice of her dress and wondered where he could pin the corsage without getting his hand smacked. Annie solved the problem for him.

"I'll wear it in my hair," she said, looking in the mirror above the dresser. "It will be perfect." When she'd anchored the orchid behind her ear, he had to agree.

If she hadn't looked so breathtaking, he might have been tempted to suggest they stay in the room and have dinner sent up, so he could tuck her into his arms while they waited.

Wrestling with his baser urges, he shrugged into the jacket of his suit and held out his arm. The male instinct to show her off warred with the elemental desire to strip off the dress like Christmas paper and uncover the treasures hidden beneath. It was going to be a long evening.

Annie's dinner was a gourmet's delight, lovingly prepared by some genius in the kitchen and presented with flair by an attentive waiter. But for all she noticed, the meal might as well have been hash from a can. Her attention was on Cole, handsome in a dark suit, a pale gray shirt and a tie striped in charcoal and teal.

He'd ordered champagne that went straight to her head, or maybe it was just his expression that made her dizzy.

"You steal my breath," he told her when they raised their glasses. Between bites he paid her more outrageous compliments. Annie chose to believe that he meant every word. He nibbled her fingers and made her laugh. He didn't even notice the knockout blonde at the next table with her parents, trying so hard to catch his eye. She pouted when he and Annie finally left, his hand splayed possessively on her bare back.

"I want to dance with you." He laced his fingers through hers. "Shall we check out the band in the lounge?"

Returning his smile, Annie could only nod. They hadn't talked much, but words seemed superfluous. She would rather read the messages in his eyes.

By the time he had escorted her to the lounge

where a three-piece group made music that flowed like warm, sweet honey, all she wanted was to wrap herself around him and hold on tight. For tonight the past was only a memory, the future an uncertain blur. The present was Cole's smile and his touch, and the light of desire in his eyes.

They found a table illuminated by a single candle, but before she could sit down he led her onto the floor. The room opened to the night and a fairy garden surrounded by trees sparkling with tiny white lights. In the center was a lighted fountain, the water spilling like diamonds into a pool below. A couple danced by, silver-haired, moving in and out of the shadows with the unique grace of longtime partners.

Fleetingly, Annie wondered at their story. Had they weathered storms together, enriched each other's lives? Given comfort and unconditional trust? Believed in each other no matter what?

Cole's hands were at her waist, distracting her from wistful thoughts. Her fingers caressed his nape as they swayed, bodies brushing, breath mingling. When the song ended, he led her deeper into the walled garden.

She turned to him willingly. His arms tightened, his mouth covered hers, hot and possessive. Her brain shut down and her senses took over, soaking him up. The tip of his tongue touched her lips, retreated, stroked again. A hum of pleasure swept through her as he changed direction, blazing a trail along her jaw while his breath teased her ear. Annie's world tilted and she clung to him, barely aware of the music or the other dancers.

"I want you, Annie-girl." His voice was rough, the veneer of sophistication stripped away to reveal the raw need beneath.

No one had ever called her by that name but Cole. Memories clawed at her with skeletal fingers, but she resisted. "Let's go upstairs," she whispered boldly.

His smile kept her warm all the way to their room. When they went inside, the curtains had been opened, the bed turned down. The lights of the city provided a golden glow.

Watching Annie move in that dress, Cole felt desire pulsing through him like the blows from a hammer. He led her to the window, his hands shaking when he kissed her. His heart thudded so hard that he thought she must hear it as she looked up at him, her face in shadow. Deliberately he slowed his hands, smoothing the silly little straps of her dress from her shoulders. Slippery as sin, it slid down her body, leaving her breasts bare except for the pendant suspended from its thin gold chain.

"You're so beautiful." His voice was a rasp he barely recognized as he cupped her face in his hands and lowered his head.

Annie threaded her fingers through his hair, holding him close. Her sigh of pleasure threatened his control. When he let her go so he could strip off his jacket and tie, his gaze wandered down her body, covered only by a scrap of sheer fabric and nylons topped with black lace. While he fumbled with cuff links and shirt buttons, she stepped out of the dress, which pooled at her feet.

The sight of her in little more than high heels and a smile was almost unbearably erotic. He'd only lost two buttons getting out of his shirt, but his belt buckle defeated him—

Annie's hands were at his waist. And in a blur of passion and need, they dealt with the rest of their clothes and sank to the bed, bodies entwined.

Loving Cole was like plunging down a water slide. Sensation after sensation rippled through Annie as he burned a trail with his fingers and followed it with his mouth. Gasping, she crested once and then again when he claimed her. Before she could draw a breath, his body shuddered and he groaned, following her over the edge.

Eventually he stirred, shifting his weight so he lay beside her. Utterly sated, Annie managed to turn her head. His eyes were shut, his features slack.

"We have to talk," he muttered, and promptly fell asleep.

Curious, but wrung out, Annie did the same.

Later, when she woke again to loving hands and a clever mouth, there was no time for words. Finally, in the pale light of morning, she opened her eyes to see him watching her with a crooked smile. Before she could speak, he pulled her close and distracted her. The shower that followed started out as a mutual seduction and ended with shrieks and giggles as the water finally turned cold.

When they had toweled each other dry and were dressing, Annie finally asked, "What did you want to talk about?" She pulled a T-shirt over her head as Cole zipped up his jeans.

"I want to keep seeing you." His head disappeared into a green knit shirt. "I was wondering if that would be a problem."

"But you live in Denver," Annie protested as her stomach launched a dive that would have made a stunt pilot proud. Was he saying that he thought they might have a future? That he still cared? Neither of them had mentioned feelings, but she knew hers were strong and true.

"I'll be coming back for Mom's wedding, and to see her from time to time. I could give you a call."

When you happen to be in town, Annie finished silently. Her shoulders sagged with disappointment. "I suppose."

Cole hadn't been able to face the idea of giving her up completely, but neither was he ready to lay out feelings he hadn't waded through. There was too much going on—with Annie, with his mother and his newfound knowledge about his biological father, even with his baby sister. He was on overload.

When he heard Annie's lukewarm response, he was damn glad he hadn't said more. She didn't sound as though she cared whether she ever saw him again!

"Great," he said with an automatic smile. "I'll look forward to it."

"Me too." She turned away, shoulders slightly hunched, and he was tempted to ask what was wrong. Instead he threw the rest of his gear into his bag.

Before they left the room, he gave it a searching look, pretending to make sure they hadn't forgotten anything. In reality, he hoped to find some clue as to what had gone so suddenly, painfully wrong between them. The last thing he saw before the door swung shut behind them was the bed, its sheets tangled as if a war had been fought there.

Walking toward the elevator, Cole felt as though one had.

When Annie pulled up in front of her office a couple of days after she and Cole had gotten back from Austin, it was with the sad realization that her part in Lily's case, except for testifying, was pretty much over. Annie switched off the engine and stared through the windshield. Even if Lily hadn't been Cole's mother, Annie would have liked her. The older woman had been through a lot in her life, but she'd found happiness with Ryan and she wasn't afraid to grab it with both hands. Their marriage was bound to be a happy one. How Annie envied them that.

Cole had a meeting with the assistant D.A. in the morning and he half expected the murder charges to be dropped. Annie wasn't so sure. The murder trial of Ryan Fortune's lover was a high-profile one. Over the past few years, Annie had heard plenty about the prosecutor. He was ambitious and he hated losing face. He'd push it to the end, hoping renewed media coverage would sweep the jury along to a conviction. Anything a member of the prominent family did was news, and Ryan's fiancée was the next-best thing to a Fortune.

One way or another, Cole's reason for being in San Antonio was coming to an end. He would return to Denver and pick up the threads of his life. Annie intended to do the same. Getting over Cole the first time had been difficult enough and she sure wasn't looking forward to going through it again.

When her name had been cleared within the police department, she'd quit the force and thrown herself into establishing her own agency. Months passed before she was able to take a deep breath; by then the pain of Cole's desertion had turned to a dull ache. This time, too, work would be her salvation.

He was coming by to pick up some paperwork, but he hadn't said when. The colleague she'd hired hadn't located Lockhart, but Rosita's husband, Ruben, heard he was still in the area. A couple of the ranch hands had run into him at a local cantina the weekend before, so he hadn't gone underground.

Annie hoped she never saw him again. Let the

police worry about building a case against him after Lily was acquitted.

It was too nice a day for such morbid thoughts. Grabbing her purse, an armload of office supplies and a potted plant, she got out of her car. Despite the gentle warmth of the sun, the hour was still early enough that the parking lot in front of her office was deserted. Both the dry cleaner and the hobby shop were closed. The burger joint on the corner didn't open until eleven.

She was about to unlock the door to the office when she dropped her keys. Juggling her packages, she bent down to pick up the key ring, and heard a car pull up behind her. The hair she'd worn loose again swung forward, blocking her vision as she groped for the keys. Her purse slid off her shoulder and hit the pavement with a *plop*.

A view of her derriere stuck in the air wasn't the picture she'd hoped to present Cole with this morning. Leaving her purse on the ground, she grabbed the keys, straightened and turned around.

"Hi, doll face. Nice to see you again." Clint Lockhart was standing a few feet away, a chilling expression on his face and a gun stuck in his belt. His gloved hands twitched at his sides.

Annie's heart thudded with alarm. Her own gun was in her purse, lying at her feet. Of all the rotten luck; could he have been driving by and just happened to see her? She'd have to brazen it out before he realized who she really was.

"How you been, sugar?" she asked, dredging up a flirtatious smile in spite of her quivering nerves. "I hope there are no hard feelings."

Lockhart's gaze shifted to the lettering on the door to her office and his hand moved up to rest on his belt next to his gun. "Can the act," he snarled. "We've got a little score to settle. You're coming with me."

Eleven

"What are you doing here?" Annie asked Lockhart, trying to keep the shock from her voice. How had he found her? What did he know?

Cars went by on the street, too far away from the parking lot to do her any good. She was on her own.

She clutched her keys more tightly as a sneer marred Lockhart's already cruel-looking face. "I never got the chance to say goodbye before Appleberry's goons ran me off the guest ranch." His gaze bored into hers. "You lied to me. That wasn't nice."

"I guess I'm just not a nice girl."

He pulled the gun from his belt and pointed it at her. Fear slid down Annie's spine as she stared at the barrel, willing herself to stay calm. Perhaps he only wanted to scare her. Unless she had no other choice, she wasn't about to take on an armed man. "You don't need that," she said coolly. "What is it you want?"

He waved the gun and her nerves jangled. How far would he go? "You were in my room, weren't you? What were you looking for?"

"Maybe I was looking for you," she drawled, stalling for time.

"Don't jerk me around. I know who you are—you're a lousy P.I. The guy at the pawnshop owes me a favor. He told me you were asking questions." With his free hand, Lockhart took a business card from his shirt pocket and waved it. "Convenient of you to leave him this. It wasn't hard to find out who you're working for, either. Just the price of a couple of beers."

Annie nearly groaned aloud. She'd hoped the man at the pawnshop might remember something about Lockhart and call her. Maybe she should have given him more than a twenty.

"It was just business. My job was to establish reasonable doubt and get Lily cleared—not to convict you." Perhaps he'd still listen to reason. "You know I didn't find anything. You aren't even a suspect, so don't get yourself jammed up here. Just climb in your pickup and drive away. I'll forget I saw you."

"Sure you will." His laugh was ugly. "No one crosses me and gets away with it." He made a threatening motion with the gun. "Come on. You drive."

"I'm not going anywhere with you!" If he got her in the truck, it would be much harder for her to escape him.

"The hell you're not." He grabbed her arm, his fingers biting into her flesh. "I'm going to—"

"Let her go. It's me you want."

Both Annie and Lockhart spun around at the sound of Cole's voice. She saw with a sinking heart that he was unarmed.

Shoving her aside, Lockhart aimed at Cole.

"Look out. He's got a gun!" Annie cried, leaping at Lockhart as a shot rang out. She knocked him off balance and his weapon skidded across the pavement.

Cole crumpled, and her heart nearly stopped. Then instinct and fury took over. Her heel connected with Lockhart's kneecap, and he screamed in pain. A couple more well-aimed kicks bent him double and her arm across his throat had him helpless.

"Cole!" she yelled, tightening the pressure, "are you all right?"

He groaned in reply, sitting up, and she nearly wept with relief. At least he was alive.

Lockhart let out a stream of cusswords as he clawed at her arm. Ruthlessly, Annie cut off the verbal abuse with his air. The bastard had shot Cole!

Behind her, the door to the dry cleaner banged open, bell ringing merrily, and Mr. Ving, the owner, came out with an automatic in one hand and his cell phone in the other.

"I called the cops," he shouted, waving the gun wildly. "Nobody move."

"Mr. Ving, it's me, Annie Jones." Reluctantly she eased up on Lockhart, who gulped air hoarsely.

"Call for an ambulance. The man helping me has been shot."

A police siren wailed in the distance. When Mr. Ving nodded his recognition and punched in more numbers, she picked up Lockhart's gun and scrambled to her feet. All she wanted was to get to Cole.

"You blink and I'll put a hole in you," she told Lockhart, pointing the gun with both hands. He was cradling his knee and rocking, eyes full of hate. His hat had been knocked off in the struggle, revealing his thinning hair.

She risked a glance at Cole, at the blood on his shirt. His face was lined with pain as he staggered toward her, holding his upper arm.

"Are you okay?" he rasped. "Did he hurt you?"

Mindful of the gun, she caught him in a clumsy embrace, babbling her thanks. "I'm fine. Help's on the way. Where were you shot?"

"My upper arm. Burns like hell, but it's just a scratch." He sat down on a brick planter, Annie close at his side.

She didn't dare trust Lockhart to her neighbor. Mr. Ving was pale, his gun hand trembling visibly as he held it at his side. At least he wasn't aiming it at anyone.

Finally two police cars roared into the parking lot, the drivers jumping out and crouching behind the open doors, guns drawn. Annie was grateful that she recognized one of them.

Keeping a careful eye on Lockhart, she held her

gun in the air and identified herself as Mr. Ving laid his gun on the ground.

In moments, it was all over. An ambulance driver who arrived minutes later worked on Cole, while Annie hovered anxiously, answering the patrolman's questions. Handcuffed, Lockhart sat in the back of a squad car, complaining loudly. In front of the building, Mr. Ving's wife was bawling him out for getting involved.

Annie and one of the officers followed Cole to the hospital, where she refused to let him out of her sight. The bullet had gone straight through without hitting anything vital, and he hadn't lost much blood, so the doctor treated and bandaged the wound.

"I'll get you a prescription and some instructions," he said after he'd helped Cole on with a sling. "You were lucky."

Annie gripped Cole's free hand, not knowing what to say. She could still hear the shot, see him fall, and she had to blink away belated tears.

"You're something," he said with a crooked grin. "Lockhart didn't stand a chance. If I had any idea how tough you are, I wouldn't have bothered stopping."

"I'm not tough," she admitted. "I was scared." She touched her hand to Cole's cheek. "You didn't even have a gun."

His hand tightened on hers. "Not part of my attorney kit." He turned his head and kissed her fingers. "Come on. I want to make sure Lockhart's behind bars."

He was waiting for his paperwork, talking to the officer, when Lily arrived with Ryan.

"My God, Cole, are you all right?" she demanded as soon as she saw him. "Annie said you'd been shot!"

"Yeah, I'm fine." He let go of Annie's hand just long enough to give his mother a one-armed hug.

"My assistant tracked me down on my cell phone," Ryan said. "What happened?" He glanced at Annie. "Are *you* okay?"

She nodded emphatically, afraid they'd blame her for putting Cole in danger. Quickly he filled them in, while they stared with horrified expressions.

"I'm so glad you're both safe," Lily exclaimed, giving Annie a hard hug.

"I feel like such an idiot for letting him get the drop on me like that," she felt compelled to admit. "If Cole hadn't shown up when he did, I don't know what would have happened." Reaction was starting to twist in her stomach like razor wire. Looking back, she had no doubt that Lockhart had meant her serious harm, and Cole could easily have been killed instead of wounded.

"The important thing is that you're both safe and Clint is in custody," Ryan said, squeezing her hand. "I can't believe this. He was my brother-in-law. But why did he come after you in the first place?"

"I think I can answer that," Cole said, glancing

at the policeman hovering nearby. "When he found out Annie was investigating him, he must have figured he was going to be arrested for Sophia's murder. He went a little crazy, holding Annie responsible, and he wanted revenge."

"Where's Lockhart now?" Ryan asked.

"In police custody, being interrogated." Cole tensed as he looked at his mother. "Maybe this will all be over sooner than we thought."

Lily's eyes filled with tears, and Ryan curled a supportive arm around her shoulders as she pressed a shaking hand to her mouth.

"So Clint killed Sophia?" he asked.

"We don't know anything for sure, but it's starting to look that way."

"I was married to his sister. He worked on the ranch," Ryan muttered, shaking his head. "I didn't like him, but I thought I knew him. It's hard to take in."

A hospital employee summoned Cole, who went over to the counter while Annie waited with the others.

"I can't tell you how scared I was when he got shot," she said, the remnants of fear still making her tremble. "He was so brave, facing Lockhart without a gun."

Lily squeezed her hand. "Cole cares about you."

An automatic denial came to Annie's lips. "It's not that," she told Lily. "Cole and I—"

"Love each other," Lily finished for her. "Believe me, Ryan and I can recognize the signs when we see them, so don't waste your breath arguing. Work out the details with my son instead."

Annie was about to sputter out another denial when Cole walked up.

"All set," he said, waving a sheaf of papers.

"Why don't you both come out to the ranch with us," Ryan suggested. "We were going to meet some friends for dinner later at The Oasis, but they'll understand when I explain the situation. You need to wind down and get some rest. Annie can stay the night."

"I'll loan you a nightgown," Lily said.

"Ryan, I appreciate your bringing Mom to see me, but now I want you to go on with your plans," Cole said with a sidelong look at the officer who was waiting patiently. "Annie and I have some business at the station. I'll fill you both in later."

For a moment, Ryan looked as though he was about to argue. Then he glanced at Lily, who was watching him with worried eyes. To Annie, she appeared brittle enough to shatter. "If you're sure that's what you want," Ryan said finally.

"I think it would be for the best."

"Are you really okay?" Lily asked him, resting a hand lightly on his sling.

Her concern seemed to affect him deeply. "Yeah, Mom, I'm fine," he replied with a reassuring smile. "I've just got some stuff to take care of."

"All right," Ryan agreed. "Come on, honey, let's leave these two to do their jobs."

"I think they've both earned more today than we could ever repay." She gave Cole another careful hug, and then Annie. "Don't forget what I said," she murmured.

"What's that?" Cole asked suspiciously.

"Nothing!" both women exclaimed as Annie's cheeks grew hot.

Was Lily right? Did Cole love her?

Hours later, Cole and Annie walked up to Ryan's table at the restaurant decorated like an opulent tent straight out of *The Arabian Nights*. The four people seated there looked up with surprise and concern on their faces.

"Is everything all right?" Lily demanded, reaching for Cole's hand.

Cole was exhausted, his arm throbbing dully, but his face broke into the grin he'd been struggling to suppress as he linked fingers with her and gently pulled her to her feet. Bussing her noisily on each cheek, he felt a lump rise in his throat as sudden, unexpected moisture blurred his vision.

"What is it?" she asked breathlessly, a smile trembling on her lips. "Good news?"

"The best. Lockhart confessed. The charges against you have been dropped."

He watched her face go pale. "Lockhart really did kill her?"

"They were having an affair," Cole replied.

"Oh, my." She turned to Ryan, who had sprung to his feet. "No one deserves what she got."

"Never mind that now," he said. "We can't help her. It's your welfare I'm concerned with."

"I'm really free?" she asked Cole, pressing her hand to her chest.

"As a bird! Thanks to Annie and her crackerjack investigating. She suspected Lockhart from the beginning." She, too, was grinning like a fool, and Cole was surprised to see tear tracks on her cheeks.

With a *whoop,* Ryan caught his mother in a hug and spun her around, laughing like a hyena. "Now we can get married!" he exclaimed, kissing her soundly.

Applause burst out around them, startling Cole. He realized that many of the restaurant patrons had been eavesdropping shamelessly. The other couple at Ryan's table leaped up to congratulate Lily and shake Ryan's hand. After he performed belated introductions, they included Annie and Cole in their good wishes.

The waiter came over and Ryan spoke to him briefly. As the other man hurried off, he raised his glass and his voice. "Champagne for everyone."

Amid the cheering and shouted good wishes, Ryan insisted that Cole and Annie join them. As soon as they were seated and trays of champagne were being circulated throughout the room, Ryan's expression sobered.

"You said that Clint actually confessed?" he asked Cole quietly.

"When the police told him they were bringing in his accomplice, Don Flynn, Clint started talking."

"What was Flynn's part in this mess?" Ryan demanded grimly. "Damn it, the man's an employee of mine."

"Flynn gave Lockhart an alibi for the night of the murder," Annie explained. "He pretended to be Lockhart when someone knocked on the door to their room with a message about a phone call. Flynn told the police he woke up and looked at the clock, establishing the time. Now Lockhart has admitted to making the call from the hotel garage. The two of them set it up."

"Why?" Ryan asked. "You mean, they actually planned to kill her?"

"I don't think so," Annie said. "But Clint was spying for Sophia. He passed on to her whatever he could about your plans, about Lily. In exchange, she'd promised him part of her settlement from the divorce, but she kept stalling. Clint was getting impatient."

"That's why he killed her?" Lily asked, clearly horrified. "Because of money?"

"Apparently so. The phone call was just to give him an alibi if anyone saw him with Sophia that night and told Ryan. With her dead, I think Flynn was too scared to come clean."

Cole was still amazed at how neatly things had

finally fallen into place when the police had questioned Lockhart. Once he started talking, they could hardly shut him up. "When he went to the hotel to see her, they argued and she taunted him. She said she'd never give him a dime. That's when he lost his temper. They struggled."

Until he'd happened on Lockhart with Annie earlier, Cole would never have understood that kind of rage, that loss of control. Seeing Annie in danger had given him a glimpse of the violent side of man. He would have done anything to save her. But of course he could never condone Lockhart's motives. The other man had been driven by greed.

"Lockhart claims he didn't realize what he was doing until it was too late," Cole added. "When he saw that Sophia was dead, he panicked. But of course, he still remembered to call Flynn."

"What about my bracelet?" Lily said. "How did that get in Sophia's suite?"

"Lockhart found it in the stable. He planned to sell it in Austin, but then he figured he could frame you or Ryan instead. He wasn't picky."

Lily stared at her fiancé with dawning comprehension. "It might have been you," she whispered.

"I'd rather it had been." His voice was low with barely suppressed fury.

"At least I had the best attorney and the best investigator around on my side," she responded.

"There's more," Cole said. "Lockhart admitted to being involved with Bryan's kidnapping, but he claims it was all Sophia's idea. Not only did she want the ransom money, but she figured stealing Ryan's grandson would be one more way to make him suffer. As if being married to Sophia wasn't torture enough.''

"So Clint knows where baby Bryan is?'' Ryan asked.

The story was so bizarre that Cole still couldn't make sense of it. ''No, that's the crazy part. Lockhart swears he didn't know they took the wrong baby until he and Sophia read in the newspaper that the one who'd been recovered wasn't Bryan. Now Lockhart claims the goons they hired to snatch him never noticed there were two babies in the nursery.''

Disappointment was etched on Ryan's face. ''And we still don't know the story behind the baby who was returned to Matt and Claudia, although he's definitely a Fortune,'' he said. ''This baby's mother has never come forward, but *someone* brought him to Bryan's christening party. That person might know where Bryan is.''

"The FBI is still investigating,'' Cole reminded him. Lockhart also denies having had anything to do with the ransom note that showed up on the anniversary of the kidnapping,'' he added. ''Lockhart said if he'd known about it, he sure as hell wouldn't have left the ransom unclaimed. The FBI wants to talk to him some more, but I don't think he's lying.''

"Why not?'' Lily asked. ''He lied about Sophia and he let me go through hell because of it.''

"If he knew anything more about the kidnapping or Bryan's whereabouts, you can bet he'd be trying to cut a better deal," Cole concluded. "But there's still plenty of reason to hope that Bryan is still alive somewhere."

"Of course there is," Ryan agreed heartily. "As soon as we get home, I'll talk to Matt and Claudia. They'll want to know the latest news. Meanwhile, we have a party to plan." He brought Lily's hand to his mouth and kissed it.

"A party?" she echoed, cheeks flushing.

"You betcha." Ryan leaned over to capture her chin in his hand. His love for her was plain to see on his weathered face. "A celebration."

When he was done kissing her and Lily had caught her breath, she beamed at Cole.

"You'll bring Annie to the party, won't you? There'd be no celebration if it wasn't for the two of you."

Cole glanced at Annie, who appeared as flustered as he felt. Sometimes irritating her was more of a temptation than he could resist. "Sure," he told his mother with a grin. "We'll be there."

"Why did you agree to attending this together?" Annie whispered to Cole, smoothing the skirt of her turquoise dress with restless strokes. Bashes like this made her nervous.

Next to Lily, the two of them were the center of attention at the huge party sprawled across the grounds of Ryan's estate. Ryan had insisted on dragging them around to meet every one of his guests, explaining each time how they'd solved the murder case and paved the way for him to marry the woman he loved. It was downright embarrassing.

Now she and Cole were posing for the photographer who'd come to take pictures for the local newspaper. Even a week after Lockhart's confession and arrest, the case was still big news.

"Can you stand closer together?" she asked as she held up the camera. "Maybe link arms."

Behind her, Cole's sister Hannah, who was holding hands with her fiancé, Parker Malone, rolled her eyes in sympathy. Annie had met them both earlier and taken an instant liking to his quiet sister.

Annie turned in time to glimpse Cole's sudden, wicked grin and a shiver of warning went up her spine. Before she could react, he leaned her over his arm. He'd ditched the sling earlier. Apparently he was a fast healer. On the way out here, he'd promised with a rakish smile to show her his scar later.

"How's this for a photo op?" he asked, and then he tipped Annie backward. She clutched at him and shrieked in surprise, but he only took advantage of her parted lips, plundering them with a kiss that rocked her to her foundation. By the time he straightened and let her go, Annie was dazed, embarrassed and furious enough to spit.

Cole's expression was unbearably smug, and the

photographer was beaming. "Terrific," she enthused.

"I want copies," Cole said.

Annie glared at the other woman. "I want that film." Then she rounded on Cole. "What the hell do you think you were doing?"

He didn't look at all repentant. "Giving in to an impulse?" he suggested. "Lighten up, Jones. Don't be a poor sport. It's a celebration."

His obvious immunity to the kiss that had scrambled her brain only compounded her humiliation. "Your reputation's intact," he added with a wink.

Annoyance and frustration bubbled inside her, but she knew she couldn't make a scene without looking like a shrew. She plastered a smile on her lips, but her eyes promised retribution.

"And your reputation's enhanced considerably," she shot back before she huffed off. She hadn't gone ten feet when an attractive man with silver in his hair approached her.

As he introduced himself and began talking in an animated way, she glanced back at Cole with a toss of her head. His grin had faded. Not for anything would she admit to him that the man was hitting her up for help with employee pilfering at the business he owned.

Cole was still watching her smile and laugh, batting her eyelashes and posturing in her skimpy dress, a glass of champagne punch in one hand, when his mother came up and gave him a hug.

"Look who's here," she said gaily.

Annoyed by the interruption, Cole turned to greet the new arrival.

"Maria!" he exclaimed, dismayed at his baby sister's appearance. She was thinner than usual and her body fairly hummed with tension.

"Hello, Cole." Even while she greeted him, her gaze darted constantly around them. What on earth was her problem? She looked ready to bolt. "Nice party." Her smile came and went so quickly that he nearly missed it, and her eyes looked haunted.

"How have you been?" he asked, conscious of their mother hovering anxiously. Hannah was moving purposefully in their direction, Parker trailing behind her. No doubt he wasn't all that eager to confront the woman who'd tried to sabotage his relationship with Hannah.

Maria gulped her drink. "I've been just fine," she told Cole. "I wish you would all quit worrying about me."

"Who's worried?" he drawled before Lily could say anything. "I've been a little busy myself lately, what with Mom's murder case and all."

Apparently his sarcasm was lost on Maria, who glanced over to where Ryan stood with a large group of friends, all laughing and talking at once. "So you still think he's going to do the right thing?" she demanded, rounding on Lily. "The Fortunes are nothing but a bunch of users. They don't care about anyone but themselves."

"Maria!" Lily gasped.

Maria gave Cole a contemptuous look. She'd always suspected his birthmark had some special significance. He dreaded having to tell her she was right. "Someday you'll wise up too," she sneered.

"What's going on?" Hannah asked, clearly puzzled.

Ignoring her, Cole put an arm around Lily's shoulders. She was trembling. "Leave Mom alone," he warned Maria. "She's been through a lot. Can't you stand for her to be happy?"

"How can any of you celebrate when there's a baby missing?" Maria's voice rose, and several people, including Annie, glanced their way.

"Will you shut up?" he growled, grabbing Maria's arm and giving her a shake. "You're making a scene."

Angry spots of temper appeared on her hollow cheeks. She wrenched free of his grip. "I'm leaving," she cried. "You're all phonies, and I don't want to be around you."

"Maria, sweetheart—" Lily started, reaching for her.

"Let her go," Cole interrupted, as Maria pushed her way rudely through the groups of people enjoying the Fortune hospitality.

Lily started to follow her, but Cole blocked her path. "I'll go talk to her tomorrow," he promised, dreading the idea. "Maybe she will be calmer then.'' He glanced apologetically at Hannah. ''I'm sorry I didn't go sooner.''

He knew with a sinking sensation that something was terribly wrong. Feeling selfish, he longed for just a short break before he had to deal with yet another family crisis.

Snagging a glass of punch from the tray of a passing waiter, he went off in search of Annie, who had disappeared. Before he took on his sister, there was something he needed to do for himself.

Twelve

In search of a few moment's privacy, Annie walked down to Ryan's well-tended rose garden. In every direction were beds bursting with exotic colors, from nearly black to the palest lavender, from cream to apricot, from pink to burgundy. Arbors and trellises were covered with blooms striped in red and white, or ones whose petals were tinted different colors. Some of the roses were fully open, while others were tightly furled and only hinting at the beauty to come. The air was pleasantly heavy with their perfume and the water from a nearby fountain made soothing music.

Annie was sitting on a low bench, absorbing the peace of her surroundings, when she saw Cole walking toward her. She had tried to work up some anger at that very public kiss he'd bestowed on her for the photographer's benefit, but found that she couldn't. If Lockhart's aim had been better, she could have lost Cole for good.

He'd be leaving Texas soon and she didn't want to fight with him. Besides, he was too breathtakingly attractive as he walked purposefully toward her now, looking very much like a man intent on claiming his woman.

The idea made Annie shiver with desire.

"You picked a gorgeous hiding place," he said as he joined her on the bench and stretched out his legs. "It's my favorite part of the grounds."

Annie was tempted to tell him she wasn't hiding. "Was that Maria I saw you talking to?" she asked.

"Yes, that was my infamous little sister, trying to spread warmth and cheer as usual."

Annie had only heard part of Maria's outburst. "Her attitude must be difficult for your mother," she said cautiously.

"I'm sure that Maria's constant and unending criticism of Ryan's family is very hurtful to Mom," Cole agreed. "That's never curbed her tongue before, but today her wild ramblings reached a new level of nuttiness."

"What do you mean?" Annie asked. She'd heard the other woman mention Bryan's kidnapping. Perhaps she'd been especially close to the baby before he disappeared.

Cole got to his feet, pacing restlessly in front of the bench with his hands in the pockets of his lightweight slacks.

"Maria has always been selfish and self-centered," he said with an edge to his voice. "Mom worries. She can't help it. I promised I'd drive out to Leather Bucket, where Maria's been living, and check on her tomorrow. Would you go with me?''

His request caught Annie off guard. ''Why do you want me to go?'' she asked. ''I don't even know your sister. Wouldn't it be better if you saw her alone?''

He stopped his pacing to look down at her expectantly. ''I'd like you to go because I enjoy your company,'' he said. ''I thought perhaps we could stop for lunch or dinner afterward on our way back. I haven't had a good Tex-Mex meal in way too long. If you want, you can sit in the car while I visit her, but I was hoping you'd go in with me. I'd like a second opinion on her mental state.''

''I don't have the credentials for that,'' Annie objected.

''I'm not looking for a medical opinion, just another observation besides my own. Granted, I'm probably not very objective after all the mean things she's said about Mom's relationship with Ryan,'' he admitted. ''But the way Maria acted today was bizarre, even for her.''

''Okay,'' Annie agreed, bending to bury her nose in a bush covered with fragrant white roses. ''Although I don't know how much help I'll be.''

Cole didn't reply, and she finally looked up to find him staring at her intently.

''What's wrong?'' she asked, glancing around suspiciously as she got to her feet. Was the photographer slinking nearby, looking for a candid shot or two? She didn't see anyone hiding behind the foliage.

Cole's gaze wandered over her. "I wish you could see the picture you make in that dress, with the flowers around you. I wish I could pick them all and lay them at your feet."

"I don't think Ryan would appreciate the gesture," she said dryly.

"The heck with Ryan." Cole's blue eyes danced with laughter. "Would you be impressed?"

"The roses you sent impressed me," she admitted. "I wish they'd last forever."

"I'll send you more," he promised, taking her in his arms.

A little quiver of reaction went through her at his nearness, and she licked her suddenly dry lips with the tip of her tongue. She could feel the tension in Cole, the same sexual tension that gripped her whenever he was near.

"Let's get out of here," he suggested, leaning forward to nuzzle her neck.

When his tongue traced a path along the skin of her throat, leaving a trail of fire and turning her good sense to mush, Annie was happy to comply.

"That's where Maria lives," Cole told Annie as he pulled up in front of a rundown trailer in a modest park. Considering how important appearances and material goods were to his sister, he was surprised she hadn't done better for herself than this desolate setting. No wonder she didn't encourage visitors. "Not very attractive, is it?"

"It's not exactly what I expected," Annie replied diplomatically. "The carport's empty. Maybe your sister's not home."

"Why don't you wait here while I knock?" he suggested. "It looks deserted." There was no shade, so he left the engine running and the air-conditioning on.

Cole climbed the rickety steps and knocked on the rust-stained door, but he was met with the silence of an empty house. Annie was right; there was no one home. Cupping his hands around his eyes, he peered through a window covered by a sheer curtain. Through it he could make out a few pieces of furniture and, surprisingly, a playpen in one corner of the main room. Through an archway he could see a high chair in the kitchen and a box of disposable diapers next to it on the floor.

Was she doing some baby-sitting on the side? He realized he had no idea where she worked. His stomach clenched as he recalled her bitter comments, her assertions that the Fortunes "owed" them. Was it possible that she'd been mixed up in Bryan's kidnapping? Could the baby things be Bryan's? Surely not. If Lockhart knew where the baby was, he would have told them—to save his own skin.

"You looking for the gal who lives there?" called an old woman who'd come out of a nearby trailer. "She ain't home."

Cole went back down the steps. "You know her?" he asked.

She studied him through narrowed eyes. "You a bill collector?"

Perhaps he should have worn jeans instead of his usual slacks and dress shirt, a tie knotted at his neck despite the heat. Habits died hard.

"No," he replied. "I'm her brother, just come out for a visit."

The woman took a drag from the cigarette smoldering between two fingers. "I ain't seen you around before. You got ID?"

With a wry grin, he pulled out his wallet and showed her his Colorado driver's license, wondering what Annie thought about all this.

"I'm from Denver," he said, while the neighbor studied the license as though she suspected its validity. He half expected her to bite it, like one would a gold coin. "See, the last name's the same. How well do you know Maria?"

She grinned, revealing stained teeth. "Not much at all," she admitted with a chuckle. "Girl keeps to herself."

Putting away his wallet, he nearly threw up his hands in frustration. Instead he managed a smile.

"Do you know where she went?" he asked with forced patience, "or when she might be back?"

"Can't say. She left a little while ago. Usually she's gone several hours, but I don't know where it is she goes."

Cole wondered if all this woman did was sit by her window and keep tabs on her neighbors. He was about to ask about the baby things he'd seen when a phone started ringing.

"That's mine," she said, hurrying off with surprising agility. "Your sis will be back in a while. Be patient."

She disappeared into the trailer, slamming the screen door behind her, and Cole walked back to the car. It was too hot to sit here and wait.

"What did you find out?" Annie asked.

Glancing at his watch, he described what he'd seen through the window and what he suspected about her potential involvement in Bryan's kidnapping. "I want to hear her explanation for the baby gear."

"A high chair and a playpen don't mean she's kidnapped someone," Annie protested. "They could belong to a friend's child. Or she could be doing some baby-sitting for extra money as you said. There may be any number of explanations."

"And I want to hear Maria's," he said grimly, stomach jumping with nerves. Maybe some food would calm it. "We passed a burger joint a little ways down the road. Let's get something to eat. Maybe she'll turn up by the time we're done and we can get a few answers.''

They were gone less than an hour. When they drove back into the park, the parking spot by Maria's trailer home was still empty. Cole wouldn't have stopped, but the woman he'd talked to earlier came out and flagged him down.

"You just missed your sister," she said breathlessly. "She showed up right after you left. I'm surprised you didn't pass her on the road."

"Did you talk to her?" Cole asked impatiently.

"I was going to tell her you'd been here, but she was in a tearing hurry. She ran inside and came out a few minutes later with a couple of suitcases." She stared at him hard. "You sure you're her brother and not the law?"

"I'm sure," Cole replied, his frustration mounting. They'd just missed her! "Then what happened?"

"She loaded her car to the gills. Looked like everything she owned. Then she locked the place up tight and took off with the baby."

He was right! "Whose baby was it?" he demanded.

The old woman looked surprised by his question. "Hers, I guess. I never asked." A suspicious expression crossed her face. "Say, what kind of family are you, if you don't even know whether or not your own sister has a kid?''

"Good question," Cole mumbled, turning away.

"Don't blame yourself for Maria's problems," Annie said after they'd left the depressing mobile home park behind. She'd heard part of what the old woman had said to him, and she could guess at the burden of responsibility a man like Cole would heap on himself.

"You know me pretty well," he said with a faint smile. "I don't even want to guess at what she's doing with a baby."

"If she was part of the kidnapping scheme she wouldn't be living in a place like that. She could name her price, and you know it," Annie told him. "There has to be some other explanation. Do you think it's possible that Maria had a baby and was reluctant to tell you?"

"It wouldn't surprise me. I don't understand her and I guess I never have," he said. "Maria was always different from Hannah and me." Cole glanced at the stereo. "Why don't you tune in some music you like?" he suggested abruptly.

Assuming he didn't feel like discussing his sister any further, Annie found a station that played soft rock. Then she sat quietly, looking out the side window at the fields they passed.

After a while, Cole surprised her by slowing

down and turning off the main highway back to San Antonio.

"This isn't the way we came," she exclaimed, puzzled. Since they'd already eaten, he hadn't mentioned stopping anywhere else. Perhaps he had an idea where Maria might have gone.

In a moment, he slowed again. "There used to be a nice shady spot by a creek down here," he said as they bumped over a narrow gravel road. It meandered past a farmhouse and a dilapidated barn before winding down a long, lazy hill toward a grove of cottonwoods. "Back in high school, my buddies and I would come here, swim if the water was deep enough, drink a few beers if we could get them, talk about the future."

Annie looked around at the rolling fields of grass in every shade of gold and brown. She wondered if he'd brought girls here, but she didn't ask.

"I won't jump to any conclusions about Maria," he promised as he eased the car to a stop in the shade and rolled down the windows. It was cooler here. "I try not to make the same mistake twice."

Annie had no idea why he had brought her here, but she could hear the faint sound of flowing water. With the long drive ahead of them it would be nice to stretch her legs for a moment.

"Can we walk a little?" she asked, glad she'd worn tennis shoes instead of sandals.

"Sure we can." He shut off the engine, yanked

his tie from around his neck and hung it on the rearview mirror. Then he released the top button of his shirt and rolled back his sleeves.

When he opened his door and got out, Annie joined him. He laced his fingers through hers. For a few minutes, they walked in silence along a path by the creek, their joined hands swinging idly. Cole seemed preoccupied, and she wondered if he was thinking about Maria again.

"The last few weeks have been like something out of a soap opera," he said finally. "Sophia gets murdered and they arrest Mom. I find out Chester Cassidy isn't my real father. You nearly get abducted. Lockhart confesses to the murder. And I find out Maria apparently has a baby."

"It's a lot to deal with," Annie agreed. "What did you mean about not making the same mistake twice?" she asked when her curiosity finally got the better of her.

Cole looked down at her as they walked. "When I leaped to the assumption that you were guilty six years ago, I lost you. It was a painful lesson."

His words shocked her to the core. "Does that mean you're willing to concede that our break wasn't totally my fault?" she blurted. She'd always assumed he blamed her entirely for what had gone wrong between them.

Letting go of her hand and turning partially away from her, he seemed to be studying something in the distance. He was silent for so long that Annie assumed her question had angered him. She didn't know what else to say. He was the one who had brought up the subject.

When he turned back around, his expression was unreadable. "I couldn't understand at the time why you wouldn't defend yourself to me," he said. "I loved you, and it hurt like hell that you couldn't confide in me. I convinced myself that you were guilty and too ashamed to admit what you'd done." He shook his head slowly. "Why didn't you trust me, Annie-girl?"

She searched his face for clues as to what he was feeling. Her own emotions were tumbling over each other like laundry in a dryer—sadness, regret, righteous indignation, pain, fear and a tiny spark of something else she tried hard to ignore.

"What's the point in opening old wounds?" she asked.

"'Until we move out of the past, the future remains a mystery,'" he recited with a crooked grin. "I read that in a fortune cookie. Pretty clever, don't you think?"

It was Annie's turn to look away. What was he trying to tell her? She wrapped her arms around her chest to control her sudden trembling. Maybe he was right and it was better to clear the air, to leave each other with a sense of closure.

"I guess it was my pride that got in the way,"

she admitted, choosing her words carefully. "My father never asked if I was taking bribes, but I know he had doubts. That hurt. When it came to you, I wanted unconditional trust, but I didn't trust you with the truth. It was unfair and I'm sorry." Her chest burned with emotion. She hung her head as tears filled her eyes.

Cole's arms came around her and he pulled her close. "Weren't we a stubborn pair?" he mused as he tucked her head beneath his chin and stroked her hair. "Each of us wanting from the other what we were afraid to give?" He dropped a kiss on her forehead and let her go. "Do you trust me now?"

He'd faced down a man with a gun for her, she thought. How could he even ask that? "Of course I do," she said. "You saved my life."

Gently he wiped the tears from her cheeks. "So that means I'm responsible for it."

"Another fortune cookie?" she asked with a wobbly smile.

He frowned thoughtfully and her heart turned over. How she loved him! "An ancient proverb, I think." A muscle jumped in his cheek. "I need to kiss you now," he murmured, dipping his head.

Annie never could resist him. She met him halfway, opening her mouth to his gentle insistence as she was drawn into the whirlpool of desire his touch always stirred in her. Finally he eased away, but his face was flushed and his eyes were dark with passion.

Her knees were rubbery and her pulse had slammed into another gear. The thought of losing him again was nearly unbearable.

"Would you come to Denver with me?" he asked suddenly. His face was all angles in its intensity, the skin stretched taut.

"What are you asking?" she nearly whispered. Was he proposing?

"Move in with me, live with me. I love you, Annie. I'm not ready to lose you again. We could give it a try, see how things go."

For a breathless moment, his words made her heart sing. He loved her! Then reality came flooding back.

"I have a business in San Antonio," she said, despair washing over her like an icy wave. "I bought a condo." Her objections sounded so silly, but to her they mattered. It hurt that they weren't important to him.

"And you're going to make partner at your firm." Her voice rose. "Your life is in Denver and mine is here."

A light came into his eyes and he gripped her arms, startling her. "Tell me how you feel," he demanded. "Do you love me, Annie?"

"Of course I do!" She gestured wildly at her

streaming face. "Why do you think I've been crying?"

"Annie, what do you want from me?" he asked.

It was time to lay her heart on the line—and damn the consequences. "I don't want just a husband for a night, like we had at the Circle A. I don't want to play house and see how it works out. I want a future with you, a real commitment, and I want my business too. I've worked hard and I don't want to start over, not again."

She turned away with a sense of real hopelessness. Now she'd done it. Instead of agreeing to the time he needed, she was pressuring him for more than he wanted to give, crowding him the way she'd heard that men hated.

Finally, when her heart was starting to crack from the strain of waiting, she risked a peek at him. His expression was grave, his eyes searching hers. "You're right, you have a great business here. Hell, even Ryan thinks you're the best investigator in Texas. I think I made a big mistake in asking you to come to Denver," he said.

Annie's heart sank like a stone. Maybe she should just go with him as he had suggested, make a new start. At least this time she wouldn't be alone.

For a moment he chewed his lip thoughtfully. "Well, I wasn't going to rush you. I thought you needed more time." He ran a hand through his hair while Annie stared, trying to make sense of his muttering.

"All my life I've been practical, organized, cautious. I've planned ahead, I've weighed and considered every step," he continued. "When it was necessary, I cut my losses and moved on. Now I'm ready to make a few changes." He gripped her hand. "Take a few chances. Maybe you're ready too."

The flutter in Annie's chest became a full-fledged churning when he sank to one knee.

"What are you doing?" she cried, hope warring with disbelief.

He looked up at her with a crooked grin. "Do you trust me enough to take a chance on a soon-to-be-unemployed attorney?" he asked. "Annie, will you marry me and live in San Antonio with me?"

"What about your job?" she cried. "You're going to make partner."

He shrugged. "I've been feeling restless for a while now. It's not the kind of law I want to practice. There's an opening for a criminal attorney in Parker's firm. I could look into it." He gave her hand a squeeze. "There's an offer on the table," he said. "Are you going to accept it?"

Annie took a deep breath, nearly overcome by the roller coaster of emotion roaring through her. "Yes," she managed.

"Are you sure?" His voice was hoarse with emotion. "If you need more time, I'll give it to you, but

I don't want to wait a moment longer than I have to. We've waited too long already.''

A flood of tenderness filled Annie as she smiled down at the man she'd never gotten over. "I'm sure."

The pressure of Cole's hand on hers increased for a moment, and he shut his eyes as if the world had grown too bright to look at. Then he leaped to his feet and swept her into his arms.

After a kiss that was more intense and moving than any they'd ever shared before, he finally let her go. To her astonishment, his eyes were moist as he gazed at her.

"You've made me the happiest man in the world," he said. "Now I want a lifetime to return the favor."

"That lifetime together can't start soon enough," Annie sighed, joy flooding through her as she laid her hand against his cheek. "This is one case I'm really going to enjoy closing."

* * * * *

Here's a preview of next month's

*Will a single mom's pretend
engagement to a handsome
Fortune heir turn into
real marriage vows in*

HIRED BRIDE
by
Jackie Merritt

"Are all of your clients unmarried?" Zane Fortune asked while looking into Gwen Hutton's lovely blue-gray eyes across the table.

Her gaze didn't waver, though she did wonder why he kept looking at her so intently. "Help-Mate was designed to assist busy people with chores they have no time to do themselves. Things a wife or husband might do if the client had a spouse with extra time. A few of them are married, or living with someone, but most are single."

"Like me." Zane took a breath, and Gwen sensed it was a preamble to something—probably his reason for delaying her departure. "Gwen," he said, "I have a problem, and I think you just might be the answer."

She became wary, concerned about the personal note she heard in his voice, and she said slowly, "I'm listening."

"I'm going to ask you something, and I hope you won't be offended, but have you ever done any escorting?"

Her eyes widened, and she started to get up from

her chair. "Mr. Fortune, if I've given you any reason to think—"

Holding up a hand, Zane broke in. "I am not suggesting anything immoral or illegal. Please don't rush into an erroneous opinion before you give me a chance to explain my question."

Gwen slowly sank back to the chair. "All right," she said flatly. "Explain." *And make it good, because if you don't I'll be crossing you off my client list!* It wasn't a pleasant thought. She needed every client she had worked so hard to obtain. Spent money to obtain, as a matter of fact. Advertising was costly, and she was always grateful when a potential new customer mentioned phoning Help-Mate because he or she had seen one of her little ads.

"What I'm going to propose to you is a simple business arrangement. I need an attractive lady to escort to a wedding this weekend. I realize there are women for hire out there, but I wouldn't insult my family and friends in that manner. Here's the situation. The females in my family have decided that I should be married, or at least committed to one woman. They have taken it upon themselves to find me a wife, and I know that there'll be at least a dozen unmarried women at that wedding just waiting to pounce on me."

"Why don't you just tell the females in your family to leave you alone?" Gwen asked with suspicion and distrust in every syllable. She had never heard a lamer story in her life. If that was Zane Fortune's favorite line, it was a wonder he got anywhere with decent women. The thing was, she enjoyed reading the society section of the newspaper and knew that Zane *did* attract decent women. So what, really, was this all about?

Zane heaved a sigh. "I wish I could do that. Actually, I've tried to do that, but it never comes off the way I'd like it to. My sisters think I'm kidding around with them, they kid back and the whole thing falls apart.

"Anyway, I came up with an idea to at least get me through the weekend relatively unscathed. Heather, my secretary, was going to attend the wedding with me, and we were going to lead everyone to believe that she and I had become an item. It's not true, of course. Heather's practically engaged. But she agreed to help me out, and then today she received a phone call from her sister in Fort Worth. Their mother is in the hospital, and naturally Heather had to go and see her."

"And you...you'd like me to take her place?" Gwen was still guarded, but she was beginning to believe that Zane wasn't handing her a line, but rather telling her the truth.

"Exactly. I'm not asking you to give up your weekend for nothing, Gwen. I'll pay you a thousand dollars if you go to that wedding with me and act as though we are *very* good friends."

She managed not to gasp, but she couldn't prevent a weakly parroted, "A thousand dollars?"

"Make it two thousand," Zane said quickly, reading her reaction as reluctance. "This is important to me, Gwen, and I'm willing to pay for two days of your time. Is two thousand enough?"

"Uh…yes. Two thousand is, uh, sufficient." Was accepting money for spending time with a man immoral, even though she would be committing no definitively immoral acts? Goodness knows, she could use the money. She lived from day to day, working herself into an early grave to make ends meet, always with that nagging worry about her children's future. With a windfall of two thousand dollars…well, there was so much she could do with it that she really wouldn't know where to start.

But just what did Zane Fortune expect for so much money?

She said what she'd been thinking, keeping her voice at an even pitch though her pulse was racing. "Before I give you an answer, Mr. Fortune, tell me exactly what you expect for your money."

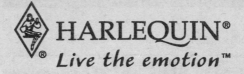

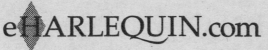

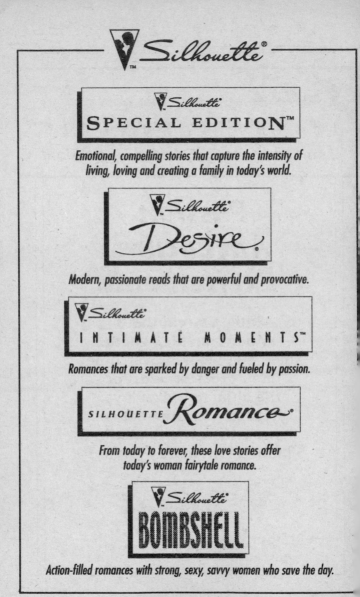

eHARLEQUIN.com

The Ultimate Destination for Women's Fiction

Visit eHarlequin.com's Bookstore today
for today's most popular books at great prices.

- An extensive selection of romance books by top authors!

- Choose our convenient "bill me" option. No credit card required.

- New releases, Themed Collections and hard-to-find backlist.

- A sneak peek at upcoming books.

- Check out book excerpts, book summaries and Reader Recommendations from other members and post your own too.

- Find out what everybody's reading in Bestsellers.

- Save BIG with everyday discounts and exclusive online offers!

- Our Category Legend will help you select reading that's exactly right for you!

- Visit our Bargain Outlet often for huge savings and special offers!

- Sweepstakes offers. Enter for your chance to win special prizes, autographed books and more.

**Your purchases are 100%
guaranteed—so shop online
at www.eHarlequin.com today!**

INTBB104R

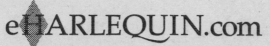